Amanda Cinelli

—

THE SECRET TO
MARRYING MARCHESI

ISBN-13: 978-0-373-13907-1

The Secret to Marrying Marchesi

First North American Publication 2016

Copyright © 2016 by Amanda Cinelli

All rights reserved. Except for use in any review, the reproduction or
utilization of this work in whole or in part in any form by any electronic,
mechanical or other means, now known or hereafter invented, including
xerography, photocopying and recording, or in any information storage or
retrieval system, is forbidden without the written permission of the
publisher, Harlequin Enterprises Limited, 225 Duncan Mill Road,
Don Mills, Ontario, Canada M3B 3K9.

This is a work of fiction. Names, characters, places and incidents are
either the product of the author's imagination or are used fictitiously,
and any resemblance to actual persons, living or dead, businesses,
companies, events or locales is entirely coincidental.

This edition published by arrangement with Harlequin Books S.A.

® and ™ are trademarks of the publisher. Trademarks indicated with
® are registered in the United States Patent and Trademark Office, the
Canadian Intellectual Property Office and in other countries.

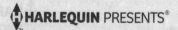

Printed in U.S.A.

Recycling programs
for this product may
not exist in your area.

ISBN-13: 978-0-373-13907-1

The Secret to Marrying Marchesi

First North American Publication 2016

Copyright © 2016 by Amanda Cinelli

Printed in U.S.A.

Amanda Cinelli was raised in a large Irish/Italian family in the suburbs of Dublin, Ireland. Her love of romance was inspired after "borrowing" one of her mother's beloved Harlequin novels at the age of twelve. Writing soon became a necessary outlet for her wildly overactive imagination.

Now married with a daughter of her own, she splits her time between changing diapers, studying psychology and writing love stories.

Also by Amanda Cinelli

Harlequin Presents

Resisting the Sicilian Playboy

For my grandmother Anne.

Who taught me to always have a pile of good
books by my bedside.

CHAPTER ONE

SHE WAS DEFINITELY being followed.

Nicole tightened her grip on the stroller's handlebar and picked up her pace. The same black Jeep had already made its way past her three times as she took her morning walk through the village. Two men sat inside, their dark sunglasses doing nothing to disguise the fact that their attention was focused entirely on her. As the vehicle slowed to a complete crawl a short distance behind her, she felt the familiar prick of ice-cold terror in her throat. It was officially time to panic.

The cobbled laneway that led up to her farmhouse was still slippery from the light April drizzle. Her ballet flats scraped against the stone as the breath whooshed from her lungs with effort. A gleeful squeal sounded from within the cocoon of pink blankets as the stroller bounced and swayed. Nicole forced herself to smile down at her daughter through tight lips, summoning an inner calm she wasn't quite sure she possessed. They were nearly home. She would lock the door and everything would be fine.

As she rounded the last bend that led to La Petite, she slowed to a stop. The gateway was filled with vehicles, and a line of cars stretched further up the lane. A dozen figures stood in wait with cameras slung around their necks. Nicole felt a humming begin in her ears as her blood pressure instantly skyrocketed.

They had found her.

Thinking fast, she pulled off her light jacket and draped it over the stroller's hood. They descended quickly, the crowd of men forming a circle around her as the cameras began to flash. She kept her head down, and the air seemed to stretch her lungs to breaking point as she tried to move forward. They seemed to gather more tightly around her. Apparently the addition of a child made absolutely no difference to the paparazzi's definition of *personal space*.

A man stepped forward, blocking her

way. 'Come on—a quick photo of the young 'un, Miss Duvalle.' He smile was shark-like, sharp-toothed and dangerous. 'You've kept this hidden quite well, haven't you?'

Nicole bit down hard on her bottom lip. Silence was the key here. Give them nothing and pray that they went away. The sudden jarring sound of a car horn was just what she needed as the black Jeep appeared in the lane behind her. The vehicle began pushing its way through the crowd, forcing the photographers to scatter. Taking advantage of the distraction, she moved as fast as she could, pushing hard through the throng.

It seemed like a lifetime before she crossed the gateway onto her own private property. They couldn't enter without breaking the law, but she wasn't so naive to think that she was somehow out of their reach.

She would never have privacy here again. The thought brought a choking sob to her throat.

She resisted the urge to look over her shoulder and focused on retrieving her keys from her handbag with trembling hands. Once she was finally inside, she slid the deadbolt into place and scooped Anna up into her arms.

Her daughter's warm cotton scent soothed her nerves, giving her a small moment of relief through the haze of blind panic. The sun shone through the windows, brightening the room and filling the space with light. Anna's sparkling blue eyes smiled up at her, so peaceful and unknowing of the situation they were in.

She needed to find out what was going on. *Now.* She gently settled her daughter on a soft mat surrounded by toys, then quickly got to work. It wasn't an easy task to fire up the ancient computer that had come with the farmhouse. One of her first resolutions upon moving to the French countryside from London had been to throw away her smartphone and stop checking the showbiz news. Still, she made sure to keep a phone charged for emergencies. One that only made and received calls—that was all she needed.

It seemed like hours before she could finally type a few keywords into the search engine on the dusty screen. She immediately wished she hadn't bothered.

'Billionaire Marchesi's Secret Love Child Uncovered!'

Seeing the words in black and white filled

her with ice-cold dread. She scanned through a few lines of the anonymous interview before turning away from the screen in disgust. Was her life always going to be sordid entertainment for the masses? She bit her lip hard as she dropped her head into her hands. She wouldn't cry.

This wasn't supposed to happen to her here. The tiny village of L'Annique had been her sanctuary for more than a year now. She had fallen in love with her kind neighbours and the quiet, almost humdrum atmosphere. Unlike in London, where her name was synonymous with scandal, here she had been free to raise her daughter in peace. And now this quiet village would be overtaken by the storm of her old life catching up with her.

Every penny from the sale of her London town house had been poured into her new beginning. Uprooting herself again would bankrupt her. And if she ran they would follow her—of that much she could be sure. She didn't have the kind of power it took to protect her child from the media.

There was only one person she knew who did. But the man she was thinking of didn't deal with idle tabloid gossip. Rigo Marchesi wouldn't even *think* of trying to help her. She was surprised the media had even dared to cross him with the sheer power of his family name. Luckily for him he had a whole team of PR people to deal with this. Nicole would be left, alone once again, to pick up the pieces and deal with the aftermath.

She parted the curtains to peer out at the crowd, frowning at the sight of the men and their cameras being herded further down the street. Two police cars full of officers had arrived and they were quickly moving all the people and vehicles down the lane and out of view.

A second black Jeep had joined the first, this one with blacked-out windows. A handful of men in dark suits stepped out and began fanning across the premises and down each side of the laneway.

Nicole felt her breathing slow to a dangerous pace, and the air rushed in her ears as she watched the last man step out of the vehicle. He was tall, wearing a sleek suit and dark sunglasses. She bit her bottom lip hard as he finally turned to face her, removing the glasses from his face. A moment of utter stillness passed before she released her breath in one slow whoosh.

It wasn't him.

For a moment there she had honestly thought… Well, it didn't matter what she'd thought. Right now the tall, suited man was walking up to her front door.

Pushing her hair behind her ears and clearing her throat, she opened the door with the latch in place, so that she might survey the imposing stranger through a comfortable three-inch gap. Something about him was vaguely familiar.

'Miss Duvalle?' He had a hawklike gaze and spoke in her native English, albeit with a strong Italian accent. 'My name is Alberto Santi. I work for Signor Marchesi.'

She felt cold humiliation prick at her memory. This was the man who did all the jobs that Rigo wouldn't lower himself to do. He wore the same disapproving glare now as he had the night he'd guided her across a crowded room, away from his employer's mocking laughter.

'I am here to help you.' He spoke calmly.

'You have some nerve, showing up at my door.' She shook her head, moving to close the gap, but found the door blocked by a polished leather shoe.

'I have orders to bring you under the protection of the Marchesi Group.'

'I don't take orders from Rigo Marchesi.' She crossed her arms in front of herself. She knew whom these *orders* were from. Knew the kind of ruthless power she was faced with here.

'Perhaps I phrased that poorly.' The man forced a smile to his thin lips. 'I have been sent to offer you assistance. May I come in so that we can speak privately?'

Nicole thought on it for a moment. It wasn't as if she had a whole lot of other options. Perhaps at least he could organise some sort of protection for them. She stood back, unclipping the latch and motioning for him to come inside.

He moved through the doorway and took in the surroundings of her simple home with quick, disapproving efficiency. He looked back down at her. 'Miss Duvalle, my team has already contained the area, as you can see.' He gestured to the men standing guard at the gateway to her property. 'We would prefer it if you had no more contact with the media until we have a chance to resolve the matter privately.'

'That's kind of difficult, considering they are camped out on my doorstep.'

'Which is why I am here. A meeting has been arranged in Paris to address this...situation. If you choose to cooperate you will be offered every assistance.'

The way he called it that—a 'situation'—made it sound like such a nuisance. A minor fender-bender in the Marchesi fashion empire's shipshape working schedule. These people had no appreciation of the fact that her entire life had been upended for the second time in less than two years.

'I have no control over this *situation*, Mr Santi, as you can see. So I doubt that I can help anyone to resolve it. All I need is to keep my daughter out of this mess.'

'The media will not relent—you know this,' he said gravely. 'Surely you expected the attention?'

'Why on earth would I expect *this*?'

The man shrugged and looked away, making it clear what he meant. Nicole felt cold shame wash over her. Just as she had on the last occasion this man had passed on a message from his employer. She shook her head in disgust. Of *course* Rigo would think that she had willingly pawned her child off to the tabloids. She was Goldie Duvalle's daughter after all, wasn't she?

Shaking off the hurt and anger, she forced herself to speak. 'Just to be clear—if I decline to come with you will the police stay to protect my privacy?'

'I'm afraid not.'

Well, there it was. She felt the skin on her arms prickle. It was clear she was being given an ultimatum. Get in the car and go and make a deal with the devil or stay put and be trapped in her home while the vultures circled.

Sure, she could always leave and find some new place. But with this much attention on them she and Anna would never live a normal life again. They hadn't managed to get a clear photograph of her daughter yet, but they would. And with the scandal of her parentage she would become infamous.

She knew what that life was like. She had lived it. And she would never put her child under that kind of microscope. But now... would she be able to ensure Anna's privacy with this scandal surrounding them both? She didn't have the kind of financial power it took to control the media, to keep her daughter's innocent face off the front pages.

Her chest tightened. Anna was too young to be aware of the drama unfolding around her. But Nicole knew better than anyone that awareness would come with age. Memories of her own childhood threatened to surface. She could almost feel the familiar stifling pressure to perform for the public.

She shook her head and paced to the window once more. The thought of those men outside, wrestling with each other to take photographs of her daughter to sell to the highest bidder... It stirred something deep and primal inside her. This was exactly why she had walked away from her old life in the first place.

She didn't want Rigo's help, but she wasn't stubborn enough not to recognise that she was in desperate need of it. She was certain he would want this whole episode erased as soon as possible. He had made his stance on fatherhood abundantly clear once already, hadn't he?

She would go to Paris. She would sacrifice her pride and ask him for help. The story would be silenced and they could all return to normality.

The European headquarters of the Marchesi Group was a gargantuan chrome-and-glass tower in the heart of Paris. It was a relatively new building, and its acquisition had been one of the first changes to his family's historic fashion brand that Rigo Marchesi had made upon taking his seat as CEO five years previously.

There had been outrage when he had moved the company's flagship building from Milan to Paris. But Rigo had a vision for the future of his company, and that vision required change.

Keeping his finger on the pulse of the modern business world was what made him a great leader, along with his razor-sharp negotiating skills and a clean-cut, dependable reputation. His unconventional choices had already seen profits skyrocket, and his family name restored after the steady downward decline of the business during the decade preceding his rise to CEO.

Great leaders were never caught by surprise. Rigo glowered at his computer screen as he stirred a spoonful of organic sweetener into his double espresso. Great leaders were not waylaid by a scandal that had apparently already been live on the internet for several hours. Above all, great leaders did not get publicly vilified by the world's media mere weeks before the biggest deal of their company's history was about to be completed.

Downing the hot coffee in one go, he stood up and paced across to the window.

Nicole Duvalle had been a blip. A moment of madness that had somehow bypassed his usually crystal-clear judgement. Rigo did not *do* mindless pleasure. He made sure that the women he took into his bed had their own careers to take up most of their time, just as he did. He was selective in his affairs and had no time for the kind of woman who was simply attracted to his net worth.

And yet when it had come to Nicole his logic had failed him. He'd got caught up in the blinding attraction between them and thought to hell with the consequences.

Well, the consequences were here now, and Miss Duvalle had no idea what she had just started.

Rigo turned as the glass door to his office opened and Alberto entered. His right-hand man looked rumpled and nothing like his usual pristine self.

'I trust your day has gone to plan?' Rigo raised a brow in question.

'She walked out after less than five minutes.' Alberto exhaled harshly. 'They offered her the deal and she point-blank refused it.'

Rigo was silent for a moment, leaning back against the desk. He'd be lying if he said he hadn't expected this outcome. If Nicole was as money hungry as her mother she would hardly accept the first pay-off she was offered. He had only offered the money to get the story settled quickly, out of the courtroom.

The deal he was currently negotiating with French jewellery icon Fournier was time sensitive. The family-owned company had been initially reluctant to merge with such a large corporation, and it had already taken months to get to this point. Rigo gritted his teeth, feeling his jaw tighten with frustration. How could one interview cause this much mayhem?

Already he had been notified of shareholders jumping ship and rumbles amongst the board members. His late grandfather had left a black spot on the Marchesi name that had almost bankrupted their eighty-five-year-old brand. After his own father's tireless work to put the business to rights, there was no way Rigo would let this shake them.

If his own shareholders were nervous, then he was damn sure Fournier were nervous, too. And he didn't blame them. Eighty per cent of their market was female. A new CEO who had apparently left his conquest pregnant and out on the street was bad for business.

Even if was a blatant lie told by a ruthless gold-digger.

'Where is she now?' Rigo asked.

Alberto looked uneasy for a moment. 'The child needed to sleep, so we put her in one of the company apartments on Avenue Montaigne.'

'She rejects the deal and you immediately set her up in luxury accommodation?' He raised a brow. 'Alberto, you are a soft touch.'

'We couldn't risk the press getting wind of her location yet,' Alberto said hurriedly.

'Forget about it. I will just have to fix this

myself,' Rigo growled, grabbing his suit jacket.

It was time for him to reinforce what he apparently hadn't made clear enough to her the last time.

He would not be made to look a fool.

Ignoring the uncomfortable burn in her stomach, Nicole scraped the rest of her half-eaten meal into the bin and poured a small glass of white wine. She needed to unwind and get rid of this nervous energy so that she could formulate a plan. A plan that did *not* involve being holed up at the top of a fancy apartment tower like a scared defenceless princess.

She walked over to the windows, looking at the lights of Paris twinkling in the dusk.

Her old life had been filled with nights like this, drinking wine and gazing out at the lights of countless beautiful cities. But no city had ever felt like home—not even London. 'Home' was what she had been trying to create in L'Annique. A stable, solid place where Anna could grow up, go to school, have her first kiss. All of those normal things that young girls were meant to go through.

And instead they'd been forced to flee, to accept help from the one man she had promised herself she would never turn to, no matter how hard things got.

She sank down onto the suede sofa and closed her eyes. It had taken over an hour to get Anna to sleep in the absence of her usual routine. She needed to pull herself together. After all, children felt their mother's anxiety, didn't they? Their entire life had fallen to pieces and she only had herself to blame.

She took a long sip from her wine and gazed anxiously out the window at the dark street below. Alberto had assured her that they were guaranteed privacy here, that they would be safe from the press until they came to an agreement. And that was all that Nicole needed right now—until she figured out what the hell her options were.

The luxury apartment was on the third floor of an exclusive building not far from the Champs-Elysées. It was all high-gloss modern minimalist furniture and white walls—not very child friendly or lived-in.

Honestly, what on earth had she been *thinking* to come here? Of course they wanted to pay her off, she cursed silently, kicking off her shoes and tucking them underneath herself. She had expected to be met with a gag order of some form, but not an outright payoff in return for her lies. She needed help, but the deal she had been offered came at a price much too high for her to pay.

She had barely thought about Rigo in the weeks before all of this. That had been no mean feat, considering she looked into her daughter's cobalt-blue eyes every single day. It had been more than a year since she had looked into the identical blue eyes of her onenight lover.

Maybe on some level she had half hoped he would be there today. She wasn't sure she would have been able to be quite so calm if he had been.

A knock sounded on the door to the apartment. Nicole stood slowly. Alberto had said no one would know her location here except for him…and his boss.

'Who is it?' She stood in front of the closed door, feeling her heartbeat pound against her ribcage.

'You know who it is, Nicole.'

She felt the deep baritone of his voice vibrate right down to the soles of her feet. She fought the sudden need to turn tail and run. She stood frozen, amazed at her own ridiculous nerves. Her stomach seemed to be flipping over in circles as she reached out and laid her hand on the doorknob.

She swung the door open and there he was. Six foot two of pure Italian male, his short dark hair perfectly coiffed to match his immaculately tailored suit.

'May I come in?' he said, the subtle hardness of his tone belying the seemingly polite request.

Nicole stepped back, opening the door wide and gesturing for him to enter.

She was aware of his cobalt-blue gaze sweeping over her as he moved into the apartment. His eyes still had the ability to make her breath catch. No doubt he was taking note of how much she had changed since they'd last met. She became acutely aware of the fact that she was about ten pounds heavier, her plain brown hair hadn't seen a stylist in over a year and she had stains from Anna's supper all over her jeans.

She self-consciously tugged the hem of her plain white cotton shirt down lower on her hips.

Rigo leaned casually against the bar in the open-plan kitchen. His arms were crossed over his impressive chest and he continued to stare at her, waiting.

'Nothing to say, Nicole?' he asked.

'I would say it's nice to see you again, but we both know that would be a lie.' She avoided his gaze, staring at a point to the left of his shoulder. 'I suppose I should be honoured that you've even bothered to speak in person.'

His brows raised a centimetre. 'Believe me, I have a thousand things I would much rather spend my time doing than this.'

'At least we're being honest.' She shrugged, telling herself not to be hurt by that statement. She had no reason to be hurt. They were practically strangers. He might be her daughter's biological father but they had only ever spent one night together. She felt heat reach her cheeks as she thought of what that night had involved.

Rigo didn't seem to take any notice of her heightened colour. 'Oh, I wouldn't say we are being honest at all, Nicole,' he drawled. 'If you're angling for more money, then I am afraid you are wasting your time. You're lucky I am offering you anything at all and not dragging you into court for slander.'

'I don't want a single cent from you.' Nicole crossed her arms defensively. 'All I want is for the press to back off and give me back my privacy.'

Rigo let out a harsh bark of laughter. 'Oh, that's your play, is it? We both know you threw away any right you have to *privacy* the moment you dragged my name through the mud.'

'I had nothing to do with this.' She met his eyes without hesitation.

'This is not a game, Nicole.' His voice took on a dangerous tone. 'I made it clear the last time we met that I am not a man to mess with.'

'I would have been quite happy never to lay eyes on you again. Your ego is so large it's amazing you can even get out of bed in the morning.' She narrowed her eyes, the anger she felt finally rising to the surface.

Rigo took a step forward, a half-smile breaking across his harsh features. 'Now, *this* is interesting. So far I've witnessed Nicole, the innocent temptress, followed by Nicole, the damsel in distress.' He raised one brow.

'But I think this passionately angry version is my personal favourite.'

Nicole was speechless. The way he looked at her, his eyes filled with such disdain… It made the hair on the back of her neck prickle. How had she ever thought that this man had felt anything close to what she'd felt that night? He was a complete stranger right now. The idea that they had ever been anything so romantic as lovers was poetic nonsense. The harsh reality was that they were simply two people who had had sex.

Once upon a time she might have thought they shared a connection. That for one night in his bed she had somehow been special.

She had been so naive.

'Rigo, you are threatening to sue me because of gossip that I have no control over.'

'Then, why have you not tried to deny it?' he countered.

'My silence is the most you're going to get. I don't deal with the press anymore.'

'You will make a public statement that the child is not mine, Nicole.'

His mere presence was so commanding that she would be a fool not to feel intimidated by the demand. She fought the emotion welling up in her chest. It was ridiculous to feel hurt at his words after so long. After all, he had made his position on fatherhood quite clear. But still, a part of her had always hoped he would come in those weeks afterwards.

Even as she'd lain in hospital, terrified to hold her tiny premature daughter, she'd held hope that his world had shifted as profoundly as hers had. That he would instinctively know he had become a father.

Indignation won out over the sadness, and she stood up a little taller, meeting his gaze head-on. 'I told you that I was pregnant with your child. You chose not to be a part of it, and that is fine. But I will *not* publicly tell lies and go against my principles as a mother just to protect your damn family name.'

He shook his head with disbelief. 'Do you honestly think I would have let you run off like you did unless I was completely sure that I was *not* the father of your child?'

Nicole walked to the kitchen counter and began digging down to the bottom of her handbag. Her fingers finally closed on the object she sought, and she turned back to meet his cold gaze once more.

'I'm telling you that you were wrong, Rigo.' She held out the photograph. 'Anna is your daughter and here is the proof.'

CHAPTER TWO

RIGO LOOKED AT the woman standing before him. She was so different from what he remembered. Gone was the carefree, uninhibited temptress and in her place was this formidable tigress of a brunette, wearing torn jeans. He always went into negotiations prepared, with adequate knowledge of his opponent. But it seemed that his previous knowledge no longer applied.

He took the photograph from her, holding it between his hands as she watched him. The picture was of a baby with soft brown curls and fair skin. He looked back down at Nicole.

'This is not proof of anything.'

Hurt flashed across Nicole's pale features for a brief instant before she shook her head and snatched the photograph from his hands. 'I don't know what else to say. I have been completely honest with you from the start. I told you that I was pregnant, and I didn't cause a scene when you chose not to be involved.'

Rigo bit his lip with frustration. She was determined to stay her course. That much was becoming brutally clear. He had known she was an actress as a child, but he had never expected her to be this stoic in her performance.

'You make me out to be such a villain in this production of yours,' he said, keeping his tone deliberately calm.

'Rigo, right now all I'm asking of you is that you use your power and influence so that I can go back home with my daughter and never bother you again.'

'And am I to presume you don't want a single penny from my heartless hands?'

She sighed audibly. 'Ask yourself this. Why would I wait almost six months of my child's life before leaking a story if I was so desperate? It doesn't make sense.'

She looked so maternal right now, so innocent. It was likely she meant to look that way—to play the victim. He shook off the feeling of unease after seeing the photograph of the child. He was here to finish this.

'You're right. It doesn't make sense.' He shrugged. 'But I am not in the least bit inclined to make sense of what goes on in your brain. Whether or not you leaked the story is of no consequence to me right now.'

'You just want me to clear your name.' She bit her lip. 'I can't do that, Rigo. I won't lie.'

Rigo fought the urge to growl. 'Nicole, I might be able to gag the media and prevent further stories, but I can't undo the damage that has already been done. The public cannot be gagged. And the only way to stop them talking is for the scandal to be disproved.' He paused for effect, watching as her eyes narrowed. 'I am willing to increase the offer that was made to you today by twenty per cent. I'm asking you to do the right thing for everyone involved.'

All trace of softness seemed to disappear as she took a deep breath, shoving both hands into the pockets of her jeans. 'As much as I want my privacy back, I can't compromise my integrity and tell a lie that will affect my daughter forever. I vowed that I would never come to you, Rigo, and I haven't until now. But right now her privacy means a lot more to me than my pride.' She looked at him, her caramel-coloured eyes wide and deathly serious. 'Do a paternity test. If it proves negative I will make whatever statement you like.'

'I fail to see the point in performing a test when I already know what the outcome will be.' He fought the urge to raise his voice. Performing a test would mean more time, and every day this scandal was out there was another day of plummeting shares.

'If you are completely sure that she is not your daughter, then you have nothing to lose.' Her voice was quiet.

'Fine—I will arrange for the damned test. But, Nicole, once the negative result is confirmed, you *will* make a statement to the press.'

'If it's negative, you have a deal.' She nodded.

'Good, then we're done here.' He made to move towards the door.

'Wait!' she called, stopping him midstride. 'We haven't discussed the details of what will be done if the test is positive.'

Rigo shook his head. 'If the test is positive...' he said, looking down again at the picture of the child briefly. Her eyes were a deep cobalt blue. If he wasn't so sure that he was sterile he might almost call them Marchesi blue.

Nicole was looking at him intently. He tore his gaze away and walked over to open the door, very intent on leaving all of a sudden.

'It would be nothing short of miraculous,' he stated plainly. 'I'm pretty sure a paternity test isn't going to change what I already know.'

With that, he closed the door behind him.

The executive boardroom of the Marchesi Group headquarters was on the forty-fifth floor. Nicole sat alone at the end of the black marble conference table while various men and women in designer suits sat around her in complete silence. No one addressed her or looked her way. She suddenly wished she could trade places with Anna, who lay happily chewing on her toes in the stroller by her side.

An elderly white-haired gentleman sat at the top of the table, watching her. Nicole cleared her throat, sitting up a little straighter in her seat. A slim leather folder was laid out in front of her. She hesitated for a moment before opening it, aware that all eyes in the room were suddenly trained upon her. The cheque inside had so many zeroes she felt her breath catch.

The white-haired man sat forward, clearing his throat. 'As the most senior member of the board present, I am presenting you with our final offer, Miss Duvalle.'

'This can't be right…' she breathed, the figures swimming in her vision.

'The Marchesi Group is offering you a generous deal in return for your public statement that Rigo Marchesi is not the father of your child.'

'This wasn't the deal.' She began to pick at her nails under the table, a familiar sense of entrapment setting in. This wasn't a meeting at all. It was an ambush.

'Understand this, Miss Duvalle. We will not be negotiating the figure on that cheque, so if you want the pay-out I would advise you to take it now.' The man sat back in his seat, openly surveying the neckline of her blouse.

Nicole crossed her arms over her chest, feeling very small and very alone in the room full of suits. It would be so easy just to do what they asked. To deny the truth and run away would be the easier option in some respects. The truth was inconvenient—just as she and her daughter were. A press release would take less than ten minutes and then she could escape. She could forget all about Rigo Marchesi and start over again somewhere new.

And what would happen when her daughter became old enough to understand? What about when she asked why her father had never played a part in her life? Her daughter would eventually find out that her mother had lied to the world and denied her the right to her true parentage.

She thought of her own mother, of her countless lies and manipulations. All for money. What kind of role model would she be if she lied to her own daughter about something so important?

She took a deep breath. These people wouldn't cow her. 'I won't be signing a thing without speaking to Mr Marchesi first.'

A woman in a beige suit spoke, her hawk-like eyes spitting fire across the room. 'I'm aware that you probably grew up observing a certain level of…legal negotiations through your mother. But are you really prepared to go toe to toe with a multi-billion-euro corporation in a courtroom?'

Nicole felt her skin prickle. These people made her feel cheap and utterly worthless.

Suddenly every other person at the table avoided her eyes, seeming very focused on the door behind her.

Nicole turned to see Rigo's hulking frame silhouetted in the doorway.

She stood, anger steeling her resolve. 'This is unacceptable. I won't be bullied.'

'I did not agree to this meeting, Nicole.' His voice was deeper than usual, and his gaze dropped momentarily to where Anna was growing rapidly more tired in her stroller. 'Go and wait in my office, I'll be there in a moment.'

Rigo stood dangerously still at the top of the table and waited for Nicole to leave before he spoke. 'Somebody had better tell me right now why this meeting was arranged without my knowledge.'

The man at the top of the table sat forward. His uncle Mario was a white-haired oaf in his late fifties, with a penchant for contesting his nephew's authority at every turn. 'We have already got agreement from the rest of the board. You have been outvoted in your plan. Swift, heavy-handed action is in the best interests of the company.'

Rigo cleared his throat, eyeing the leather-bound folder on the table and closing it with a loud snap that resounded across the table. 'This will not be buried with legal settlements.'

A brave PR executive spoke up. 'You know that this company's past makes it far more vulnerable to the media. Your father always made it clear that private indiscretions cannot be allowed to fester.'

Rigo felt his patience snap. 'My father is no longer CEO of this corporation. *I am*. Everyone who is not a member of the board leave the room. *Now*.'

He turned to the window, taking three deep breaths as the men and women quickly scurried from the room. This afternoon had pumped his adrenaline into overdrive—and only half of it had to do with suddenly finding out about this clandestine meeting.

He turned to face his uncle, the only board member present. 'You don't have the power to make my decisions for me, Mario. If you wanted my job you could have fought for it.'

'I value my free time far too much.' Mario rolled his eyes. 'This is a straightforward pay-off, Rigo.' He stood up, stalking towards him. 'This woman is slandering the Marchesi name out there and jeopardising the entire Fournier deal, for God's sake.'

'It's not slander,' Rigo stated gruffly, hearing the words echo in his mind as he said them. 'I had the DNA analysis confirmed twenty minutes ago. The child is mine.'

Mario was silently stunned for a moment, his mouth agape. 'You agreed to a paternity test without alerting the legal team?' His eyes bulged. 'Are you completely insane? Even your grandfather wasn't that stupid.'

Mario didn't seem in the least surprised at the news itself—which was more than could be said for Rigo. He was still absorbing the information. His brain was working overtime, examining the revelation that, against all the odds, Nicole had been telling the truth. He had never once wavered in his certainty that she was lying. He'd long ago taken very permanent measures to make sure he would never be put in this position again. And yet here he was.

His uncle cleared his throat, looking pointedly at the leather folder. 'Marchesi men have all committed some indiscretions, Rigo. It seems it is a family weakness. My advice is to not let this get in the way of resolving the matter. Everyone has a price. Find hers.'

Nicole paced from one side of Rigo's open-plan office to the other. Her fists clenched by her sides as she weighed up the options in her head.

Plan A was to walk out of there without another word to Rigo Marchesi *or* his goons. She could take her chances with the press and beg for privacy—or, more likely, just give up on her dreams of ever having a normal life again. But her daughter would grow up knowing that her mother had tried her best.

Plan B... Well, plan B was to take every moral she had and throw it out the window.

She sat down on the nearest armchair and tried to clear her thoughts.

Strangely, she wished her mother were here to guide her through this. No, she corrected herself, she wished that her mother cared enough to try to help. But Goldie Duvalle was a law unto herself, breezing in and out of her daughter's life in between marriages and even then only when she wanted something.

The last time she had seen her mother had been the day she'd told her that she was pregnant. Cold anger made her fists clench tight by her sides, her insides tightening at the memory of having her last thread of hope pulled out from under her. Her mother was not an option—not unless she needed some contacts for a magazine spread.

With her own upbringing to go by, maybe she had been fooling herself to think she could offer her daughter a normal life. Her erratic childhood had been the furthest thing from normal you could get. It seemed that scandal was just destined to follow her around everywhere that she went.

She looked around, feeling small and alone in the iron-and-marble-dominated office space. Anna had fallen asleep in her stroller by the window.

Rigo entered the office with a dull thud of the heavy panelled door behind him. His usually perfectly groomed dark hair was ruffled, and that same formidable expression on his face made her confidence waver.

He stood still, looking around him. 'The child?'

That one question caught her off guard. She frowned, gesturing to where the stroller sat by the window, her daughter now sleeping peacefully inside.

'She won't wake if we speak?' he asked.

Nicole shook her head once, trying not to soften at his apparent concern. 'She's a deep sleeper, thankfully. She should be fine.'

Rigo nodded brusquely, his eyes lingering on the pale pink blankets for a moment before turning back to her. His eyes held the strangest combination of anger and some other unknown emotion.

They stood there for a moment, facing each other in complete silence, before Rigo finally spoke.

'Let me make it clear that I had nothing to do with that meeting.' His jaw was tight as he held her gaze in earnest. 'The board members were growing impatient and decided to act against me. I'm sorry you were put through that.'

She hadn't expected an apology. It kind

of threw her. 'I told you I wouldn't sign anything without the test.'

'You did.' He breathed out heavily. He walked past her, moving across the large office to his desk. He gestured to a leather wingback chair, motioning to her to sit, and taking a seat behind the desk once she had.

With his hands clasped in front of him he looked instantly more powerful and infinitely less approachable. The formidable CEO, taking care of yet another item on his agenda. He was powerful and unyielding, and yet right now he looked off balance somehow.

'I have received a phone call from the laboratory,' he said calmly. He tapped his thumb absentmindedly on the desk. He looked at her. 'The test results reveal a positive DNA match.'

Nicole stared back at him for a moment, unsure of what to say in response to this sterile, emotionless statement. 'I see,' she said quietly, watching as his thumb continued to move of its own volition, beating a steady rhythm.

'That is all you have to say?' he asked.

She shrugged, biting down on her lower lip. 'I already knew what the result would be.'

He leaned back in his seat and watched her thoughtfully for a moment before speaking. 'I chose not believe your claim based on what I believed to be the facts, Nicole. Now that I know I was mistaken… Well, our current situation is regrettable.'

It was like speaking with a corporate drone. Was it simply 'regrettable' that he'd missed the first six months of his child's life? Nicole thought of the countless milestones that had come and gone, the days and nights full of laughter and tears. It seemed as if an entire lifetime had passed between them since the day he had made his *regrettable* choice.

Anger flared in her chest as she took in his solemn expression.

Rigo continued, oblivious to her inner turmoil. 'The media's attention is an immediate concern for us both, but I feel that we can come to an agreement to work it to our advantage.'

She crossed her arms, amazed that he was still talking business when he had just found out he had a daughter. 'I've told you already. I won't lie to the press to save your public image.'

'I am not asking you to lie,' he countered. 'Now that I know she is mine, I do not plan to deny the fact. Publicly or otherwise.'

There it was. The words she had hoped to hear a lifetime ago. Only instead of feeling relief that her daughter would have some sort of relationship with her father, all she felt was cold, icy fear.

She stood up, taking a few paces away from him. 'First of all, she is not *yours*,' she said breathlessly, turning back to face him. 'You are biologically her father, but the rest you have to earn. I am not asking for anything right now other than your help in getting the press off my doorstep.'

He didn't speak. He just watched her with that same intensity she had come to recognise was naturally him.

Nicole crossed her arms, looking down at him. 'There is no obligation for you to play a part in Anna's life if you don't want to.'

'We both know that my walking away isn't an option here.'

She didn't know if that meant he didn't want to walk away or that he knew it wouldn't look good. She had a hard time believing that it was completely the former.

'I would be happy for you to play a part in her life. But if you go public as her father you know that I will be hounded by paparazzi for the rest of my days. Pictures of her will be used to pad out every tabloid on the planet. Is that what you want?'

'You don't want to lie, but you don't want me to tell them the truth?' He sat back, his eagle eyes surveying her with keen interest. 'It seems we have run out of options, then.'

'All I'm asking from you is media protection,' she said calmly. 'I know such things exist with your kind of power.'

'Protective orders are flimsy and easily overturned. The photographers would still come for pictures of you. The story is out there and she will always be a child of scandal. It will stick to her like glue.'

'There has to be a way…' Nicole felt herself weaken with the weight of his words. He was right, of course. The damage had already been done. Scandals like this never truly disappeared.

Had she really been so naive as to think that he could somehow magically make it all go away? She had brought her daughter into this world and made a vow never to let the same things happen to her that she had suffered herself as a child. Being hounded by cameras at the school gates and constantly playing a part for the media. She had grown up far too quickly as a result. How could she let her daughter suffer the same?

Rigo cleared his throat, standing and coming around to perch against the side of his desk. 'There is a way, Nicole. One I'm prepared to offer so that we might work the media to our mutual advantage.'

'How on earth could we do that?' She looked at his serious expression, feeling utterly defeated. She had only made things worse by running away and hiding. Anything she did now would just be damage control. A normal life wasn't something the secret child of a billionaire could ever hope for, was it?

Rigo's voice was cool and businesslike. 'The fastest and most effective way to turn a story on its head is to give the media an even bigger story to salivate over.'

'What could be bigger than this?' She frowned.

'A wedding. To be more precise, *our* wedding.'

Nicole was silent, hardly believing what he

was saying. If she had heard him correctly that was absolutely ridiculous and not a real solution at all.

'You want to pretend that we're *married*?' she said incredulously. 'That wouldn't do a thing—everyone would know it was a sham.'

'I am not suggesting a sham.' He looked down at her, some unknown emotion blazing in his eyes. 'Nicole, the only way to end this scandal once and for all is for me to prove that I have not abandoned my child and her mother. To make a grand production of how wrong the media has got it. And the best way for me to do that…is for you to actually become my wife.'

Rigo watched as the colour drained from Nicole's face. She wasn't wearing a scrap of make-up, the dark waves of her hair were tied at the base of her neck, and yet she still looked effortlessly elegant. She was frowning at him, her brown eyes wide with shock.

Not the reaction he had expected.

'You can't be serious,' Nicole whispered.

Rigo crossed his arms, looking down at her pale face. 'That's not what a man expects to hear when he has just proposed marriage.'

'You haven't proposed anything. You've just thrown another deal at me. One that I am not prepared to accept under any terms. I'd rather take the money and run.'

'I assure you that I am completely serious. And this isn't just about business—not now that I know I am a father.' He almost stumbled over the simple word—a word he had never intended to label himself with. 'Nicole, like it or not, you and I and Anna are now irrevocably linked together. I am simply suggesting that we make that link public and permanent so that we might solve all our problems at once.'

'I can't believe that you are actually prepared to marry me to save your precious business.' She let out a single shocked burst of laughter.

'This would be a legal union—a real wedding. What I'm proposing is a way to secure and protect both our interests. Now that I know I have a child, I will want to play a part in my daughter's life.'

'Would that still be the case if your precious shares weren't decreasing?'

Rigo felt the barb hit him and instantly tensed. 'I might not have planned this, Nicole, but I would never turn my back on my own flesh and blood.'

She lowered her eyes, wrapping her arms around herself in that defensive gesture she always seemed to use when she was around him.

Finally she cleared her throat and looked back up at him. 'It *is* possible to co-parent without being married, you know.'

'I was lucky enough to grow up with the love and support of both of my parents in one home. I had private schooling and medical care along with overall financial stability. Are you telling me that, given the choice, you wouldn't want the same for Anna?' He narrowed his eyes. 'What is your alternative?'

Nicole looked down at the ground, biting on her lip. They both knew what her alternative was. Rigo knew after tracking her down that she didn't own a home. She had already made a big move to a new country in the past year.

'There is a lot more to parenting than money, Rigo. I may not know where my career is going right now, and I may have had to budget, but I am a good mother. I love my daughter more than anything on this earth.'

She swallowed hard and he caught a glimpse of moisture in her eyes before she blinked it away.

'I wanted her from the moment I knew she was there. That's more than I can say for you.'

Rigo had no argument for that. He was trying to convince her to do the best for their child when he had already done the worst thing a father could do by not being a part of her life. He had started this conversation as a means to an end—a way to solve a problem in the fastest and most efficient way possible. But suddenly he felt the weight of his proposal hit him.

He was proposing to acquire a whole *family*, not a company. The thought almost unnerved him, sending shivers down his spine.

Clearing his throat, he hastily continued, 'If we marry she could have the best of both.' He chose his words carefully. 'Nicole, think of this logically. We have a child together and we both need this scandal gone as soon as possible. We need a long-term solution that puts Anna first.'

'Stop with all the business jargon, for goodness' sake.'

She walked away from him, and for a moment he feared she might walk out through the door. But he could tell by the way she glanced at him from the corner of her eye as she stared out the window that she was on the ropes. He was a skilled negotiator. He knew when to go in for the kill and when it was best to let his opponent have some breathing room.

He remained silent as she seemed to wage a battle within herself, her hands wringing together tightly. Eventually she turned back to him, her expression unconsciously giving away all her thoughts.

'I've sacrificed everything to ensure my child has the best life I can give her. And now it will never be the same, no matter what choice I make.'

'Then, you have everything to gain by marrying me.' Rigo took two steps forward—just enough so that he could see her face clearly.

'I can't believe I am even considering this.' She looked up at him, dropping her hands to her sides. 'I don't believe in these kinds of… nonmarriages. It's absurd.'

'Marriage is not a belief system, Nicole. It

is a union between two people to protect mutual assets and interests. You told me to stop treating this like business, but that's exactly what this would be.'

'How can you be so cold and logical when you're proposing to shackle yourself to a woman you have already made it clear you see as nothing but a gold-digger?'

'Your past will be forgotten so long as you commit yourself to being a respectable partner for my public image.' Rigo shrugged.

Nicole's eyes widened. 'How utterly romantic.'

'If you imagined flowers and love letters, I'm afraid I won't be that kind of husband.'

'This is all very overwhelming, Rigo. Three days ago I was living a quiet, normal life. Now you are asking me to voluntarily put myself back into the media circus…'

'You would have to deal with their judgement either way. Why not do it on your own terms for once? In this world our lives are just one big game to the public. Sometimes we are forced to choose whether to play or be played.'

CHAPTER THREE

NICOLE LOOKED UP at the man who was offering both to save her and ruin her all at the same time. What kind of woman would she be if she agreed to such a marriage? She knew exactly what kind she would be. One just like her mother.

Except her mother had never chosen her husbands based on the interests of her daughter. It had only ever been about money and magazine spreads. Nicole had simply been another instrument to use in her love affair with the media.

'If I were to agree to this, I would want your word that Anna will never be a part of your public image. She will never be used for photo ops or anything of the sort.'

'She will be protected. You have my word on that.'

Nicole nodded, swallowing the ever-growing lump forming in her throat. Her hands were trembling. The enormity of what she was agreeing to threatened to unravel what was left of her composure completely.

'We can agree on the finer details in good time. For now, am I correct in assuming that you are accepting my proposal?'

Nicole took a deep breath. 'Yes, I will marry you.'

Triumph gleamed in his eyes and he nodded his head once in approval. '*Bene*. I will call a meeting with my PR team and get the ball rolling.'

He held the door open for her before striding ahead out into the large bustling atrium of the top floor.

Nicole frowned. That was it? She had just agreed to marry him—surely they had more to discuss? Their living arrangements...the backstory for this ridiculous charade.

She followed quickly behind him, all the while feeling as though her head was no longer attached to her neck. She was doing the right thing, surely? This was the best course of action for her daughter. It didn't matter that she was essentially selling her life to this man in return. It was a business arrangement. He would likely be gone most of the time and she would be free to carry on raising her daughter in peace.

'Rigo—wait.' She reached out, bringing them both to a stop. 'I need to know what happens next. This is all very fast.'

'I will take care of it. You just need to worry about playing your part.'

Nicole felt the coldness of his words right down to her toes. Unable to speak, she nodded her head, avoiding his eyes.

Rigo began tapping his phone. 'I'll have you both moved into my apartment immediately. You can give a list of the items you need from your old home to Alberto.'

'We will be living together so soon?' Nicole asked, dipping down to look in at Anna, where she still slept peacefully in her stroller.

'We will need to get started on our united front right away. We will let the press know that we have nothing to hide.' Rigo turned around, entering into a hushed conversation with his right-hand man and effectively cutting her off.

Nicole tried not to balk at his complete lack of interest in interacting with his daughter. She needed to curb her expectations here. There was no point in expecting anything close to normal from this arrangement. It was enough that Rigo had proposed marriage to protect their child. She wouldn't dare to hope for anything more from him.

Rigo stayed as long as possible at the office before returning to his apartment. The ninth-floor penthouse in the sixteenth *arrondissement* had been his first purchase as CEO five years ago. It boasted a wide-open rooftop terrace and a sweeping view of the Bois du Boulogne. An ideal space for the little leisure time he took—the perfect blend of modern decor and 1930s vintage features to suit his taste. Although almost everything was made of hard edges and high gloss—not exactly the ideal place for a small child to roam about.

Listening for a moment, he was relieved to hear no noise coming from the bedrooms. Nicole and the child had been moved in early in the afternoon and he had purposely waited until well after dinner to return. He'd needed time to think, to process this monumental shift.

The living room held no signs of change

at all. Everything lay just as he had left it that morning. It was a bachelor pad of the highest order, with a large black marble bar dominating one side of the dining area and a flat-screen television mounted in pride of place above the fireplace. Had it really only been fourteen hours since he had downed his coffee while watching the morning news? He had walked out through the door just as he had every other day, sure that he had everything in his life under control.

Nothing could have prepared him for those test results.

There had never been a single doubt in his mind that Nicole was chancing her arm at palming her pregnancy off on her richest conquest. Money-hungry admirers came with the territory when you were a Marchesi. He'd had enough experience of gold-diggers to last him a lifetime.

And now he was a father.

The thought hit him on the chest with heavy finality. He could sit there all night and brood, while getting painfully intoxicated, but that wouldn't solve anything. It would only serve to leave him with a raging headache, and the issue of fatherhood would still be there in the morning.

He had long ago made a difficult choice, knowing that one day he would be able to reverse it if he so wished. But he had never once expected it to reverse itself. His doctor had assured him this afternoon that it was extremely rare. 'Natural reversal'—that was what he'd called it. Rigo called it mutiny. He had become quietly accustomed to the idea of never having a child of his own. The decision to have a vasectomy had been both necessary and final.

What were the chances? The one night he had forgotten to use a condom... A night that he had never been able to forget...

Nicole Duvalle was the exact kind of woman he had spent the past ten years avoiding like the plague, and yet he had taken her to his bed without a second thought. That night he had thrown caution to the wind and taken what he wanted for once. For a brief moment in time he had believed that maybe he could be someone other than who he was. Being with her had unleashed a thirst inside him for something more than the rigid confines of his world. And then he had found out who she was and that thirst had disappeared with crushing finality.

She had been like a drug to his numbed senses. In a world of falseness she had seemed so real and pure. He had drowned in the intoxicating attraction that had burned between them, losing track of time. If his right-hand man hadn't intervened and told him who she was...

He walked to the window, looking down at the inky darkness of the Bois du Boulogne. It didn't matter what might have happened. It didn't get much more complicated than this. He was engaged to marry a woman with a reputation murkier than most politicians. She had raised hell through the tabloids for most of her adult life and she was only twenty-five. Nicole swore that she was a changed woman and that she wanted nothing from him or the media. But he knew all too well how a woman could lie.

Feeling tiredness seep into his bones, he made the decision to choose his usual eight hours' sleep over a night of wallowing in the past. He walked down the hall to his bedroom, pausing when he noticed the decidedly feminine articles of clothing draped across his bed sheets. The bathroom door opened and Nicole emerged, her hair wet from showering, covered by only a short bathrobe.

She jumped when she saw him, standing completely still in the doorway.

Rigo's breath hitched. The scent of warm vanilla and honey was reaching across the room to tease his senses.

Nicole pulled the belt of her robe tighter around her small waist, the movement only serving to push her breasts out further against the thin fabric. Rigo clenched his fist by his side.

'They put all my things in here with yours.' She spoke quickly, avoiding his eyes. 'Your housekeeper was very…excited.'

'I see.'

Rigo briefly took in the two perfectly toned creamy thighs below the bathrobe and felt the tension in his muscles increase. His gaze must have given away some of his thoughts, because Nicole cleared her throat and quickly grabbed her clothing from the bed. Without another word, she slipped back into the bathroom to dress, closing the door behind her.

Rigo leaned back against the dresser, feeling his breath hiss out between his teeth. This was an unforeseen complication in an otherwise perfect plan. His staff was from the best agency in Paris, but nothing was truly confidential in his world. They were presenting the media with a whirlwind love story. It was expected that he should share a bed with his new fiancée. As any red-blooded man would.

He had thought that seeing her for who she was would effectively erase whatever it was that had drawn them together that night. Clearly his body had other ideas.

He undid the buckle of his belt, sliding it out from its loops and coiling it up into a tight spiral as he walked across the room. His walk-in dressing room was of the highest specifications, with personalised nooks and cabinets for every little detail. Organisation was his secret pleasure. Seeing everything perfectly lined up gave him a sense of calm.

He opened his belt drawer to find it only half filled with his own items. The second half contained an array of colourful scarves. Frowning, he opened the next cabinet, to find that completely rearranged, too. His housekeeper had clearly taken a shine to Nicole, he thought with an uncomfortable prickle of foreboding. If they were expected to share a bed, of course they would be expected to share closet space. He felt as if he had jumped head first into a rabbit hole and there was no going back.

He abandoned his dressing room with a scowl, returning into the main bedroom to find Nicole dressed in simple pale pink linen pyjama trousers and a white tank top. She was gathering her things into a small case, a frown marring her brow.

'All your things have been put away in my dressing room.'

His voice came out harsher that he'd intended. Nicole looked at him incredulously.

'Is that somehow *my* fault?'

Rigo raked his hand over the growth of hair on his jaw, his mind wrestling with the myriad implications he hadn't foreseen. 'We will need to share a bed until this wedding is over with,' he gritted, removing his tie and folding it up on the antique dresser. 'We can't risk the staff spreading rumours.'

Nicole's brow rose. 'That's not happening.'

'What's wrong? Afraid you won't be able to control yourself?'

He watched as she bit hard on her lower

lip, looking away from him. When she looked back he was surprised to find anger in her expression rather than embarrassment.

'This isn't what I agreed to, Rigo.' She stared at him. 'It's not…appropriate for this arrangement.'

'Believe me, I am *not* a threat to you. I'm counting down the days until this wedding is over just as much as you are.'

'Well, then, why on earth would we need to sleep together? Surely you trust your own employees?'

'I make it a rule not to trust anyone.' He began to open the buttons at his neck, noticing how her eyes followed the movement. 'We are supposed to be in a whirlwind love affair here. We will share a bed. End of discussion.'

'It's nice to see that I have some say in this arrangement.'

'About as much of a say as I do, *cara*,' he drawled. 'Sleeping alongside each other is the least of our worries right now.' He removed his shirt, folding it up before moving to unhook his trousers. He looked up to find Nicole watching him.

She cleared her throat as if to speak, but

no sound came out. He almost smiled when she averted her eyes, sliding quickly under the covers and pulling them up to her chin. He might have won this round, but who was the real winner when the prize was a night of physical torture?

Rigo finished undressing, opting to leave his boxers on. He usually slept completely nude, but he decided that might be a step too far in this cosy little arrangement. He lay down, crossing his arms behind his head. Her breathing was slow and contained, but he could sense the tension coming off her in waves. They both felt it—the madness they were capable of unleashing if they let their guards down.

He was in for a long night.

It took a moment for Nicole's mind to adjust when she awoke in Rigo's bed the next morning. Holding her breath, she turned to find the other side of the bed empty. The sheets were still warm, so he hadn't been gone long. Sleeping next to a wall of half-naked muscle had seemed an impossible task last night, but in the end she had slept soundly, having been so exhausted from the day's events.

The apartment was quiet. Anna had woken once briefly for comfort in the night but had fallen back to sleep in the crib that Rigo had arranged to be transported from her home along with the rest of her things. While she still slept Nicole took her time to shower and apply light make-up, silently thanking the staff's efficiency in having all of her belongings transferred from La Petite so quickly.

The thought of her beautiful farmhouse being occupied by new tenants made her heart break. All the little homely touches she had added would be removed and painted over…all trace of their time there gone. That life was just a memory now.

She'd agreed to this marriage for Anna—to give her a relationship with her father and a better life than she could offer. But still something plagued her. It was almost as though she had got away from the ever-present threat of the media only to be presented with another, less obvious threat in Rigo.

She was glad when Anna finally awoke so that she could focus on the usual routine of her day and avoid the uncomfortable thoughts that played on her mind. But she soon found that 'normal' wasn't so easy to achieve with a housekeeper anticipating her every need. A breakfast buffet was presented to her, along with an array of freshly prepared baby meals for Anna. Fresh fruit, crêpes, pastries and steaming coffee filled the kitchen island.

Nicole thanked the woman for her thoughtfulness. The food was much better than the simple meals she had learned how to prepare in La Petite. She had never cooked more than toast for herself before moving away from London, having always eaten in trendy restaurants and cafés in order to be 'seen'. But surprisingly learning to cook and bake had been a secret joy of hers while she was pregnant, along with cleaning and just being self-sufficient.

Sitting here and seeing that all of her baby's bottles had been washed and steamed, all of their clothing laundered and pressed… It made her feel strangely redundant. She felt a deep frown settling between her brows and instinctively smoothed it away.

'Nicole, the nannies are here to be interviewed.' Alberto's tall, thin frame appeared in the doorway, startling her.

'Nannies?' Nicole swallowed a mouthful of melon and stood up to face Rigo's right-hand man. 'I never arranged for any interviews.'

'Rigo made a shortlist from the most elite agency in Paris.' He smoothed his shirt absentmindedly, clearly bored with the day's task.

'I didn't agree to a nanny,' Nicole argued. 'This is something he should have cleared with me first,' she said quietly.

'I'm just the messenger. Take it up with him if you have a problem,' he droned.

She bit her lip and picked up her mobile phone. She would call him and calmly tell him that it was not okay for him to commandeer her life simply because they were going to be married. She took a breath, then paused, suddenly realising she didn't actually have her fiancé's phone number.

Alberto rolled his eyes at her request, pressing a button on his own phone and handing it to her. Nicole avoided the older man's cynical gaze. He made her feel deeply uncomfortable any time he was around. The memory of him silently escorting her out of this apartment all those months ago had never truly left her.

She was shaken from her thoughts as Rigo's deep baritone answered with a curt, *'Si?'*

'Did you arrange for someone to care for my daughter without consulting me first?'

A shuffling of papers could be heard in the background, along with hushed talking before he spoke to her again. 'Yes, I arranged for a selection of candidates to arrive this morning. As I'm sure Alberto has already informed you, seeing as you are calling me from his phone.'

'Why would you presume that I need help, Rigo? I've cared for her just fine for the past six months of her life—or do you think me incapable?' She heard the hostility in her voice, but didn't care.

Rigo sighed on the other end of the line. 'Nicole. You will have a handful of events to attend and an entire wedding weekend to get through. I hardly think walking down the aisle with the child strapped to your back will be practical, now, do you?'

Nicole bit her lip, absorbing his words. She had been so caught up in the storm of changes that she hadn't even thought of who would care for Anna. She had never needed anyone to watch her daughter before now, having spent all her time at home with her. Perhaps she *did* need someone trustworthy— just until the wedding was done with…

'I'll take your silence as an apology,' Rigo drawled on the other end of the line. 'Is there anything else you would like to accuse me of this morning, or will that be all?'

'No, that was it,' she said quickly, her cheeks burning. 'I'm sorry for presuming that you thought—'

'Don't worry about it.' He cut across her, and the sound of voices became louder in the background. 'I have to go, but make sure you are ready at seven this evening.'

'Ready? For what?' She frowned.

'We're going to dinner.'

With that the call ended, and Nicole looked unbelieving at the device in her hand. He had just demanded she be ready at a certain hour—was that how this arrangement was going to go?

Alberto coughed pointedly in the doorway and she rolled her eyes. 'Yes, all right. I'll be in in a moment.'

She handed him his phone and breathed a sigh of relief once she was left alone in the kitchen for the first time. Anna sat in her high chair, happily sucking on a piece of buttered toast and watching her intently.

'What on earth have I got us into, baby girl?' she whispered, brushing a tendril of dark hair behind her daughter's ear.

Anna's answering gurgle was completely incoherent, as expected, and yet it made her smile. She knew that the key to getting through this wedding alive was to focus on her daughter every step of the way and put her own needs last.

If only her future husband didn't seem so intent on making everything so difficult.

'Isn't this a little flamboyant?' Nicole's eyes widened as she took in the gilded sign above the restaurant door. 'We could have spoken in private in the apartment just as easily.'

'The food is good here, and we need to be seen in public.' He guided her inside, speaking briefly to the hostess and angling them both slightly away from the line of guests at the door.

It shouldn't surprise her that a man with Rigo's taste and reputation would choose to take her to the most exclusive restaurant in Paris. The two-hundred-year-old building was situated right next to the gardens of the Palais Royal and was one of the finest Michelin-starred establishments the city had to offer.

The hostess ushered them to a private dining room and introduced them to their own personal maître d' for the evening.

The restaurant was one of the few in Paris that she had never eaten in before. The waiting list was impossibly long and she'd only ever visited before on short trips. There was no way Rigo could have got in at such short notice, even if he *was* a billionaire. Unless he'd already had this table reserved for tonight...for dinner with someone else. The thought did strange things to her stomach.

Biting her lip, she focused on the stunning decor that surrounded them as the waiter laid down their napkins and filled their crystal glasses with iced water. Ornate golden mirrors lined the walls of the dining room and neoclassical frescoes adorned the ceiling along with stucco garlands and roses.

'I'll admit I've become a little jaded by gourmet food of late, but Le Chef Martin is one of the best in Paris.'

Rigo gestured for Nicole to peruse the

menu, and in the end they agreed on a *menu plaisir*—a bespoke sample menu designed by the chef himself.

Nicole allowed her glass to be filled with a fragrant golden wine. She was aware of her empty stomach and limited herself to only one small sip, feeling the smooth liquid warm her insides instantly.

'We will be throwing an engagement party in three days.' His deep voice interrupted her thoughts. 'The process is going to be very fast and intense, so my PR team will want to brief you about interacting with the press.'

Nicole gulped. 'Is there really a need for all this fanfare? It seems to make more sense for an arrangement like this to take place in an office or something.'

'A large wedding is expected in my family. Anything to the contrary would draw suspicion,' he said, making it clear that the issue was not open for discussion. 'We will be married at an exclusive secret location on the first of the month.'

'That's less than three weeks away.' She felt her fingers tighten on her wine glass. This was all of a sudden becoming so much more than the simple solution she had agreed to.

'Why the frown? You will be the star of your very own fairy tale, Nicole. I had thought you would be jumping for joy.'

'Because I'm so fame hungry, right?' Her temper threatened to flare but she curbed it, taking a small sip of wine. 'If it inflates your ego to think I'm overjoyed to be marrying you, then by all means please continue.'

Rigo sighed. 'We will need to find a way to stop this enmity if we hope to convince people this is genuine.'

'I'll just draw upon my mediocre acting skills, shall I?'

'I'm serious, Nicole. There is a lot at stake here for both of us. The press is not going to be gentle.' He raised a brow. 'But I'm sure you've grown a tough skin over the years.'

'I've been given no choice.' Nicole sat back in her chair, crossing one leg over the other and casually smoothing out her dress across her knee.

'So why run away from them in the first place?' he asked. 'Why not sell your story straight away?'

'Instead of selling it now, you mean?' She squared her shoulders at his veiled comment.

'Is that why we're here? For you to try to make me confess my crimes?'

Rigo shrugged. 'I'm just trying to make sense of the woman I'm set to marry.'

'Well, you clearly already have me tarred, so forgive me if I don't feel like pleading my case.' Nicole felt the shame of his accusation wash over her.

'You're not on trial here, Nicole. Whether or not you leaked that story makes no difference to me. I don't *need* to trust you.'

'Good, because I will never trust *you*,' she countered.

'Well, then, this is an excellent start to any marriage.' His laugh was entirely false as he took a sip of his wine and continued to survey her with that cool blue gaze.

'I'm sure we will live happily ever after,' Nicole said drily. She wished she were back in the apartment watching Anna sleep rather than sitting here under his scrutiny.

'Ah, there's that sarcasm again,' Rigo said harshly. 'We may not be traditionally happy, Nicole, but we owe it to each other to make things tolerable at least. We're in this for the long run after all.'

Nicole sat up straight in her seat. 'Just how long do you plan to stay married?'

'We are barely engaged and you are already planning the divorce?'

She felt his comment like a slap in the face. 'I'm aware that you see me as a cheap copy of my mother, Rigo. Please stop insulting me.' She cleared her throat and looked away from him, refusing to show any sign of the emotion that was bubbling under the surface.

'Look at me. That is not what I meant.'

His hand on her wrist turned her back to him, the contact sending a thrill of electricity up her arm.

'*Per l'amore di Dio*, everything I say is not a deliberate attack on your character.'

'You have made presumptions about my character since the first time we met. At least be upfront about your opinion of me and then maybe we can move on.'

'You want me to be honest? Fine.' He sat back in his seat. 'When I first saw you in that ballroom I pinned you as yet another husband hunter, joining the pack. I didn't know your name but I knew your type. Desperate to be noticed. You were everything I deliberately avoid, and yet…I couldn't take my eyes off you.' He took a sip of his wine, keeping her pinned with his eyes as he continued to speak in that low, husky tone. 'I kept seeking you out in the room, listening for your laugh. It was irritating, and damned infectious, and it made me desperate to know what the hell was so funny.'

Nicole remembered looking up into those deep blue eyes for the first time, being pinned by the infamous Marchesi blue gaze. She had already been far out of her depth and she hadn't even known it.

'You entranced me, Nicole. It's rare that I do anything without a second thought. But with you... I don't think either of us did much thinking after that first dance.'

She felt his gaze sweep over her features, down past the neckline of her dress. It wasn't leering or inappropriate, the way he looked at her. It was the same way he had looked at her that night all those months ago. As though she were a work of art that his eyes needed to worship and savour. As though she was the singularly most beautiful woman on the earth.

She bit her lip, calming the rage of hormones that seemed to have risen within her.

It must be a combination of the wine and being out for the first time in a long time, she argued with herself, and nothing to do with the magnetic male presence across the table from her.

'And now look—it seems I've caught myself a husband after all.' She raised her glass in a mock toast, desperate to steer the conversation back to safer waters.

'If that were true you might possibly be the most forward-planning woman in history.'

His words were intended as jest, but Nicole could see a hint of speculation in his eyes.

They were interrupted by the arrival of the first dish: the chef's specialty, *pâté en croute*. Nicole took her first bite and stifled the urge to moan. This was so more than just food. It was a work of culinary art. It made the tension of their conversation melt away as the food took over.

The meal passed slowly from there, with the chef changing the wine with every new dish. In typical French style they took their time—food in France was an event after all.

Rigo asked politely about her life in L'Annique. She told him about her farmhouse, La Petite, and the relatively quiet life she had led. Her heart mourned the loss of the secluded paradise she had created for herself and her daughter. The daughter he hadn't even held yet...

By the time the waiter had finished clearing away their fifth tasting—a dish of succulent lobster claws on a bed of warm rhubarb—Nicole was feeling thoroughly indulged and refused the offer of a dessert platter. Rigo agreed, dismissing the waiter, who removed himself swiftly, leaving them alone.

'I have something to give you,' he said.

Nicole watched as Rigo reached into his jacket pocket and retrieved a small grey lacquered box with a single silver rose painted on top. She had been in Paris on enough occasions in the past to know that the box came from Fournier, one of the most expensive luxury jewellery boutiques in the city. She felt her stomach clench tightly as he laid it on the table in front of her.

Without a word she eased open the top and took a moment to survey the glittering diamond ring that lay within. It was huge. The large white diamond virtually dwarfed the rest of the platinum band, which was encrusted with more sparkling gems.

'This looks…very expensive,' she offered, not exactly knowing what else to say as she laid the box back down on the table.

'I gave it to you to put on, Nicole. Not to decorate the table.'

When she didn't make an immediate move he leaned forward, taking the ring out of the box and offering his hand to her. She placed her hand in his and watched as he slid the band slowly onto her third finger. The stone was so large it bumped her knuckle.

Rigo surveyed the end result before releasing her hand. 'Now. You are officially my fiancée.'

Nicole looked up at the man she had agreed to join her life with and tried to resist the urge to scratch at the band so tightly clamped on her finger. Biting her lip, she swirled the remaining wine around her glass a couple of times.

A phone beeped. Rigo pulled a sleek black device from his pocket and frowned at the screen. 'The press have arrived. I had our location leaked.'

'They're here?' Nicole breathed, looking around as though expecting cameras to start appearing from the walls.

He nodded. 'Outside. It's time for us to leave.' He stood and motioned for the waiter to retrieve their coats.

Nicole wrapped her light jacket around her shoulders, hurrying to catch up with his long strides. Rigo stopped just before the open doorway, turning to her and taking her hand in his. His skin was hard and warm on hers and he stood so close she could smell the scent of aftershave on his skin.

'All you need to do is act naturally.'

Nicole nodded, her insides quivering at the familiarity of the situation. 'Act naturally'—what a paradoxical phrase. There was nothing *natural* about this relationship...nothing to help her feel comfortable by Rigo's side. She had done this a thousand times—waited in anticipation before playing her part for the press. Only this time she wasn't alone.

Rigo stepped forward, and the dull hum of the crowd outside travelled through the air. She barely caught a glimpse of the first flash before Rigo's head suddenly descended, his lips covering hers in a kiss that took her breath away. Momentarily stunned, Nicole didn't dare to move as his scent enveloped her, his warm muscular forearm sliding around her waist to hold her against the hard planes of his abdomen.

His lips grew more demanding as his tongue demanded entrance, sliding hot and hard against hers in a sinfully erotic rhythm. His other hand swept her hair back and rested against her cheek, the heat of his palm seeming to scorch her. She moaned low in her throat as she finally began to give in to the delicious sensation—only to have Rigo break the kiss just as quickly as it had begun.

His voice was low and husky in her ear as he turned them both to face the wall of cameras. 'Make sure they see the ring.'

CHAPTER FOUR

RIGO BRACED BOTH hands on the marble countertop of the master bathroom. Taking a deep breath, he exhaled in one long burst in an effort to alleviate his tension. That kiss had been planned because he knew a candid shot would get them on the front page. But his reaction had taken him completely by surprise.

He was stressed—that was the only logical answer for a grown man having to fight off his libido after one kiss. Even as a hormone-addled teenager in boarding school he had been the most rational and in control of his peers.

Scowling at his reflection in the mirror, he decided a long cold shower was in order, to clear his brain. He unbuttoned his shirt and folded it neatly into the linen basket, doing the same with his trousers. He had just removed his boxer shorts when the door to the bathroom swung open unexpectedly.

Nicole's eyes lowered, taking in his state of undress briefly, before she spun on her heel to face the other way.

'Oh, God…I'm sorry!' she groaned, covering her mouth with her hand.

Rigo fought the urge to laugh at her innocent reaction to his naked body. She was far from a shy virgin—that much he knew for sure.

'Nothing here you haven't seen before,' he drawled, taking pleasure from her evident discomfort. 'There's no need to play the maiden.'

'I'm not playing anything.' She breathed in deeply. 'And it's not appropriate for you to keep…alluding to events in the past that we both want to forget.'

'Does it unsettle you to think of our night together?' He took a couple of steps forward, the urge to reach out and draw her against him again was almost painful.

Nicole turned around to face him, crossing her arms over her chest in a gesture that couldn't say have said 'no' any louder if she had screamed it.

'It's better if we don't talk to each other that way, that's all,' she said, keeping her eyes trained firmly above his chin. 'I just need to get my things and I'll go to the other bathroom.' She gestured to the items spread haphazardly across the countertop.

'No, I'll go.' Rigo moved past her in the doorway, noticing her body tense as his arm brushed hers. It seemed she was wound just as tightly as he was.

'Thank you.' She quickly gathered her nightclothes from a drawer, disappearing into the bathroom without another look back at him.

Rigo abandoned his plan for a cold shower, deciding that maybe a cold Scotch might serve him better. He had just eased a pair of loose-fitting sweatpants over his hips when a loud bang came from inside the bathroom.

'Is everything okay?' He paused, his fingers on the handle.

The sound of rustling fabric and a delicate female grunt could be heard through the thin panel of wood between them.

'Do you need help?' he asked, hoping to hell that the answer was no.

'I'm fine,' she called out, but her breathing was definitely laboured.

Moments passed before the door opened and Nicole appeared dressed in a simple pink nightie. Her hair was deliciously ruffled, and Rigo tried to look away—but not before he noticed an angry red welt snaking down her shoulder blade.

'*Madre di Dio*, what happened in there?' Rigo looked past her, noting the bottles of lotions and potions scattered along the counter and on the floor in disarray.

'Nothing, I just slipped. I think I ripped my dress,' she said sheepishly, holding up a pile of red fabric.

He reached out, touching the reddened skin on her shoulder. 'I'm more worried about your arm than the damned dress. Would you honestly rather risk splitting your head open than ask for some help?'

'Who knew independent dress removal was so dangerous, huh?' She shrugged away from his touch. 'I'll survive, I reckon.'

She moved past him, hanging up the torn dress. 'I would try to sew it myself, but I'm terrible at anything that requires precision.'

'That doesn't surprise me.' He pointedly eyed her shoes on the floor.

'What exactly do you mean by that?' She placed a hand on her hip.

'You've unleashed a minitornado in my bathroom, for one.' He gestured to the array of bottles and brushes scattered all around his usually pristine bathroom.

'That's different. I fell. But I just don't care if everything is lined up correctly. I've noticed *you* are freakishly neat. I'm almost afraid to touch anything in the closet.'

'I like organisation.' He shrugged.

'Well, I am more organised chaos.' She grabbed a pair of fluffy pink socks, slipping them onto her feet.

It was strange, seeing her this way. He didn't think he'd ever seen a woman in actual nightwear. But then again, he'd never lived with a woman before. He'd spent the night with former girlfriends, of course. But none had ever gone without make-up, and their nighties had left a lot less to the imagination.

Nicole's cheeks were flushed from her scuffle with the dress zipper, the rest of her skin flawlessly pale against the contrast of the dark waves of her hair. The nightie she wore skimmed just across her knee—hardly an instrument of seduction. And yet the sight of her full breasts curving against the soft cotton made his libido roar to life once more.

'This is the kind of thing that can end a marriage, you know,' Nicole joked, intruding on his less than innocent thoughts. At his puzzled look she continued, grabbing her hastily discarded shoes from the floor and looking for a place for them. 'My mother left her third husband because he chewed too loudly.' She shook her head. 'She said it made her want to poison his food.'

Rigo raised a brow, watching with trepidation as she moved a few items around in the walk-in closet area. 'So my tidiness will be the cause of our divorce?' he asked.

'That's if I don't drive you insane with my mess first.'

'You seem very fixated on the eventuality of our marriage ending,' Rigo said, watching as the smile died on her lips.

'Why would you have had a prenup arranged if you didn't expect a certain outcome?' she countered, stepping out of the closet and closing the door behind her. 'I've been to enough of my mother's weddings to know not to be naive. Marriages end, Rigo. It's just the way things go sometimes.'

Rigo moved towards her. 'And when this inevitably ends, what will you do then?' he asked, surprised that he genuinely wanted to know the answer.

'Will I move on to another rich husband like my mother did, do you mean?' She pondered for a moment. 'Or perhaps you are the beginning and end of my illustrious career?'

He stepped closer, angry at her for once again twisting his words. But he soon realised his mistake. He stood still, feeling the pull of her scent, seeing the telltale dilation of her pupils as she looked up at him. He could just take her to bed and let them both give in to this angry heat between them. She wanted it just as badly. He could tell by the way she moistened her lips with the tip of her tongue.

His hand trailed along her jaw. Their bodies were separated by a mere inch of space. Her hands came to rest on his shoulders, small and pale against his olive-toned skin. He encircled the indentation of her waist, feeling the smooth curve under his fingertips. He wanted nothing more than to tear every piece of clothing off her and see if his memories of her naked body were simply an exaggeration of the brain.

Three long breaths passed with them both standing still before she finally stepped away. He almost groaned with the mixture of relief he felt mingled with crushing disappointment.

She pushed a tendril of dark hair away from her face. 'This is just a result of us being forced into close quarters.' She sat on the bed, tucking her fluffy sock–covered feet underneath her. 'I'm going to sleep.'

Rigo blinked, trying to convince his body to follow the same path as his mind. There was no way in hell he would get to sleep anytime soon. His breathing was still heavy—as was hers. He could see the flush on her cheeks as she lay down and pulled the covers hurriedly over herself.

'I've got some work to do,' he said gruffly, needing to put some distance between himself and her beguiling presence. 'I'll likely be gone tomorrow before you wake, but Alberto will be on hand if you need anything.' He left the room, trying not to dwell on the way her skin looked, so pale and inviting against the black sheets.

Why her ease in laying down boundaries should bother him, he didn't know. He had done the same thing, hadn't he? He should be grateful that she wasn't blatantly pursuing him to try to gain more leverage in their situation…

An impromptu trip to New York had taken longer than anticipated, making it almost a week before Rigo stepped back on French soil. Having already changed into his evening suit on the jet, Rigo entered the apartment with barely ten minutes to spare before they were scheduled to leave for their engagement party.

The middle-aged nanny stood in the living room, holding Anna in her arms. The baby was smiling, clearly content in the older woman's arms.

'Monsieur Marchesi.' With a smile she walked over to him, gesturing for him to take the child from her arms.

Rigo shook his head. 'I've actually got a call to make.' He made to move away, but the woman just smiled and placed the child gently in his arms before he could protest further.

'I'll be back in a moment.' She looked down at the little girl. 'Just look how happy she is to be in Papa's arms.'

Rigo was frozen as the nanny disappeared into the kitchen. His arms felt awkward. The child barely weighed anything and yet he felt as though he held a solid boulder against his chest. What was he doing here? This was exactly why he'd been avoiding the apartment. He should have just collected Nicole at the door, as he'd planned.

Anna looked up at him with blue eyes just like his own, full of curiosity. She reached out to grab the shining satin of his tie, pulling it out of place and frowning. She was a serious child. Rigo felt an urge to laugh at her tenacity, but breathed out with relief as the nanny finally returned, holding a bottle of milk. He returned the curious blue-eyed bundle to the woman, murmuring something about his call, before stepping out to the peace and seclusion of the terrace.

He leaned forward on the balustrade, feeling the breath hiss out from between his clenched teeth. The evening light was fading and a handful of stars were emerging in the sky above the iconic Eiffel Tower in the distance. Normally this spectacular view would calm him after even the most hectic of days. But at that moment it did nothing to calm the quiet demons of his past threatening to escape from the corners of his subconscious.

He had thought his biggest problem was keeping his own inconvenient attraction to Nicole at bay, but it seemed he had entirely avoided coming up with a plan to deal with the fact that he was a father. His daughter was a Marchesi through and through—that much was now clear. Whether or not he had ignored the similarities at first, he wasn't sure. But in the handful of times he had seen her since she'd arrived in his life he had become increasingly drawn to her.

He had meant it when he'd told Nicole that he planned to play a part in his child's life. But as to how to begin playing that part, he had no idea. How did one apologise to an infant for missing the first six months of her life?

Rigo ran a hand across his jaw, feeling the tension in his muscles weighing down on him like lead in his bones. All he had to do was get through the next few weeks until their wedding was over. Then they could set about living separate lives. Perhaps that would be better for the child than having a virtual stranger unsettle her by trying to play daddy.

He shook his head, banishing all other thoughts from his brain. He had to be on the ball tonight. This engagement party was a chance for the company to publicly put the rumours to rest. Three hundred high-profile guests would be joining them to celebrate their union, and the Marchesi Group would be front and centre, taking the opportunity to capitalise on the exposure.

His plan had been a success from the moment the first picture of their kiss had hit the tabloids. Pictures of Nicole's ring had gone viral and she had been immediately scrutinised, with full spreads about her past as a child star and her subsequent struggles as an actress being dug up. But for the most part the spin had been a positive one. The media was abuzz with this unexpected turn of events, and the company's shareholders had immediately seen dollar signs.

For a fashion house there really was no better publicity than their figurehead's very public no-expenses-spared wedding. His own team had taken full control of the event, with him only having to sign off on venues and entertainment without much of a second glance. The date had been booked and the paperwork prepared. Once tonight was through, the whole world would be on tenterhooks, waiting to follow Europe's most talked-about couple down the aisle.

Having never previously allowed the press access to his personal life, he'd be lying if he said it wasn't intrusive. But it was necessary. Once their wedding had passed they would revert back to making selective outings as a couple, keeping Anna under a complete protection order from the media.

'I wasn't sure you were going to arrive.'

Nicole's voice drifted from behind him and Rigo turned, his eyes widening as he took in the beautiful woman standing in the open doorway. She was breathtaking.

The dark waves of her hair were swept back to one side in a fashion that reminded him of old Hollywood. Her eyes seemed sultry and more intense, and a luscious red colour enhanced her full mouth. His throat slowly dried as he appreciated the way her light blue dress seemed to showcase every single delicious curve of her body. He vaguely recognised it as one of the exclusive pieces from their upcoming haute couture autumn line—an exquisite concoction of powder-blue lace and shimmering crystals. The overall effect was mesmerising.

His pulse quickened as he noticed the provocatively sheer panel that ran from the middle of her thigh to just below her knee. He cleared his throat, realising she was looking at him expectantly and he hadn't yet spoken.

'I would never stand my fiancée up.' He looked down at his watch. 'When I said seven I didn't mean it with military precision.'

'It's hard to be late with a team of make-up artists and hairdressers.' She smiled. 'Thank you for organising that, by the way.'

Rigo shrugged. 'You need to make an impression tonight.' He looked down at those endless legs once again, feeling his jaw tighten in response. 'We need to leave now.' He brushed past her, momentarily surrounded by the sweet scent of her perfume before powering across the living room to the doorway. Nicole took a moment to speak with the nanny before following him with a puzzled look in her eyes.

He didn't care if she was upset at his lack

of pandering compliments. This might be their engagement party, but it wasn't a date. And the less comfortable they were around each other until their wedding was over, the better.

Nicole held her breath as the car pulled to a stop. Bright lights flashed rhythmically against the one-way windows. Rigo finally ended the call he had been on for the entire journey just as the chauffeur opened the door.

Plastering on her best smile, she stepped out behind her fiancé, accepting his arm as support as they headed into the fray.

Cameras flashed from all directions as they stopped on the bottom steps of the hotel to pose for the photographers. Questions were fired at them in loud streams of French, Italian and English. Some were innocent, enquiring about their upcoming nuptials and about the dress she wore this evening. But one particular journalist took no time in going in for the kill.

'How does it feel to have nabbed a billionaire, Miss Duvalle?' she asked acidly. 'Your mother must be very proud.'

Nicole kept her smile frozen in place, ignoring the attempt at provocation. Her skin prickled where Rigo's hand lay at the base of her spine. She stole a glance at him. He was effortlessly casual, wearing the same smile he used for all the press. They were directing questions at him, too, mostly about the recent jump in sales of Marchesi prêt-à-porter range and the subsequent rise in stock prices. No one asked *him* about his sexual past, or made assumptions about his character. They treated him like a person. They respected him.

She focused on smiling for the cameras, moving her body so that they got good shots of the dress.

'You seem very covered up, Nicole.' A young male journalist smirked. 'Has your fiancé decided to take your risqué dress sense in hand?'

'Do you still have an alcohol problem?' another called out.

'How do you plan to shed all that baby weight for your wedding?'

Nicole swallowed hard as the barbs kept on coming. The PR team had been clear on the questions they should answer and the ones they should ignore. But it seemed the more that she ignored their assaults, the harder they pushed.

Rigo just sailed through without a scratch, but she felt as if she was fourteen again, being thrust in front of the paparazzi like a juicy steak to a pack of starving dogs. They all wanted a piece of the golden widow's daughter. They wanted her to be just as scandalous as her mother.

'What about the baby, Nicole? Who gets the magazine spread for little Anna?'

Nicole froze.

'Who asked that question?' she called out, unable to control her response.

Her voice was drowned out in the sea of noise. Rigo held her arm tighter, trying to steer her further along the line, but Nicole stood firm.

'Who was it?' she asked again, her voice a little louder. 'There will be no talk of my child—do you understand?'

She was vaguely aware of Rigo's hand sliding around her waist, her body being turned towards him before his mouth was next to her ear.

'Smile and walk, Nicole,' he whispered harshly, his breath fanning against her neck.

She shivered in response, her teeth scraping her bottom lip as she fought the mad urge to nestle against him and drown out the poisonous din that surrounded them.

She gave one final wide smile before letting Rigo guide her away from the flashes and up the wide stone staircase of the hotel. Once they were safely inside and away from prying eyes, he turned to her with barely controlled frustration.

'You almost lost it out there,' he warned, his voice a low rumble. Anyone walking by would think they were lovers, whispering sweet nothings to one another.

'I held it together,' she said quietly.

'Barely.' He reached a hand under her chin, forcing her head up to look at him. 'You need to practise your poker face.'

'You're saying it doesn't affect you when they speak your daughter's name? When they talk about her as though she is a commodity to be speculated upon?'

'It's their job,' he gritted. 'You need to grow a thicker skin.'

Nicole shook her head in disbelief. Of course he didn't care about Anna. All he

cared about was how this sham of a relationship affected his stock prices.

She stepped back from him, letting his
hand fall from its place on her chin and re-
gaining a little of her composure. 'I just don't
want them talking about my child. I don't
care what they think of me.'

She walked past him, powering ahead towards the elevator that would take them to
their party on the top floor.

Rigo fell into step behind her. 'Maybe just
try to pretend that you're happy to be here?'

Nicole fought the urge to roll her eyes, pin-
ning her best smile back in place and focusing on maintaining as little physical contact
with her infuriating companion as was hu-
manly possible.

Once they reached the opulent grand ballroom and greeted their A-list guests, that task
became significantly more difficult. With
each new introduction Rigo took to draping
his muscular arm lightly around her waist in
a display of confident possession. His seduc-
tive smile and hooded looks were certainly
for show, and yet she felt her pulse quicken
with every change in the pressure of his fingers through the lace of her dress.

A man stepped casually in front of her, leaning forward to drop a light punch on Rigo's arm. Nicole stepped back, the gesture catching her off guard. Rigo didn't seem fazed at all by the action. In fact he practically beamed as recognition dawned.

'*Fratello!* You made it after all.' He turned to embrace the man, clapping his hand roughly around his shoulders. After a moment he stepped back, circling his arm around her waist once more. 'Nicole, this is Valerio—my brother.'

Nicole offered her hand and a polite smile, trying to ignore the coldness in her future brother-in-law's gaze. Apart from the blue eyes, the brothers were very different. Rigo was tall and athletic, whereas Valerio was more hulking and broad. But they definitely shared the ability to make a woman feel thoroughly disapproved of.

'I thought at least *one* member of our family should be present at your big announcement.' Valerio turned back to Rigo without another glance in her direction.

'Will your parents not be joining us tonight?' Nicole turned to Rigo.

'They're currently on a schooner cruise in

the Indian Ocean,' he explained. 'They will return in time for the wedding.'

Nicole nodded, biting her lip. If his brother was openly disapproving, she dreaded to think what his mother would be like.

Nicole looked around at the throng of people staring at them, their hushed conversations and averted looks doing little to disguise their blatant curiosity. They were all wondering the same thing: Why were they here? It was public knowledge that Rigo Marchesi was a self-professed bachelor. Now all of a sudden he had a fiancée and a six-month-old daughter and the world was supposed to not blink an eyelid. The ridiculousness of it suddenly became too much. She needed a drink—or three.

Rigo watched as Nicole made her way across the room towards the bar. She had excused herself politely but he had felt the tension building in her from the moment they'd entered the room. She was on edge—but then so was he.

'So, your fiancée...?' Valerio's smile didn't quite meet his eyes as he took a long sip of his whisky. 'What has it been? A whole week of courtship?'

'What can I say, little brother? When you know, you know.' Rigo shrugged.

'This whole situation is like history repeating itself. Are you sure the child is even yours?' Valerio lowered his voice.

'I'm not even going to grace that question with an answer.' Rigo's jaw tightened.

'I know you haven't told Mamma yet. Just because they're in the middle of the ocean doesn't mean she hasn't got a satellite phone glued to her side.'

'I thought it best to wait until they had finished their trip.'

'You're afraid to tell her.' Valerio smirked. 'I would be, too. After you jumped into proposing to the last one.'

Rigo felt every muscle in his body tense at his younger brother's reminder of a time when he had been younger and infinitely more naive. He resisted the urge to throw him down and fight it out, as they had as boys. Maybe he would postpone that for the future…in a less crowded place.

'No more talk of that—not tonight.' Rigo motioned to a waiter to bring him another drink. 'We are here to toast my beautiful fiancée.'

He raised his voice so that the men and women surrounding them joined in, thus cutting off their intimate conversation.

Taking a deep breath, Nicole ignored the heat flushing her cheeks and stopped to take a glass of champagne from a passing waiter. It didn't take long for her company to be monopolised by the other guests. Everyone wanted to know more about the woman who had finally snared the elusive Rigo Marchesi.

Rigo's PR team had advised her to stick to the essentials and avoid awkward questions about their time apart. After a few minutes she felt her nerves melt away. Suddenly she found herself almost enjoying the pretence. She talked about her fiancé with the compulsory flowery endearments, referring to their relationship with all of the expected love-struck excitement of a newly engaged woman.

After the third time reciting the story she almost started to believe it herself.

How wonderful would it be if this were actually true? She sipped from a flute of champagne and listened as the group of women surrounding her gushed about her ring. What would it be like to be actually engaged to Rigo Marchesi? If this had truly been a celebration of their love with their closest family and friends? What would it be like to be the woman who held all of his attention?

As she began to describe their fictional proposal story for a fourth time she became aware of a commotion at the doors of the ballroom. A woman burst in, her shrill voice cutting across the soft music of the jazz band.

'This is *my* daughter's party, you buffoon!' she exclaimed in a thick London accent, turning a hasty smile on the crowd of hushed guests. 'Look at your bloody list again.'

A guard quickly appeared beside Goldie Duvalle, speaking in hushed tones into her ear. Whatever he said made her ageing features twist with distaste.

As though in slow motion, her mother's trademark red talons lashed out and struck the guard on the jaw.

Nicole prayed for the ground to open up and swallow her at that moment. She looked across the ballroom to Rigo, watching as he nodded briefly to the security guard. The man backed away, clutching his red cheek, as Goldie scanned the crowd and easily spotted her.

'*There* you are, my love.' She rushed forward in her sky-high heels and her daringly low-cut neckline, crushing Nicole into a dramatic embrace.

'Mother, what are you doing here?' Nicole kept her voice low, pulling away from the obnoxious display of maternal affection.

'I'm here to celebrate your engagement with the rest of these people.' Goldie smiled brightly. 'I'm going to presume my invitation got lost in the post and speak no more of it.'

Nicole cleared her throat, silently thanking the band for playing a louder tune to smooth over the awkward interruption. 'I didn't invite you, and you know why.'

Goldie's eyes narrowed a fraction. 'Let's not give in to dramatics on such a wonderful occasion, my love.' She took Nicole's hand in her own, squeezing it in a ridiculously maternal gesture. 'I decided it was past time to make up after our little spat. I wouldn't want to miss my only daughter's wedding over a silly misunderstanding.'

Nicole felt her jaw clench. A *misunder-*

standing? She strengthened her resolve not to lower herself to her mother's level. She was the hostess tonight after all, and she had to play her part.

'If you want to stay—fine. I'm not going to draw any more attention to you by kicking you out, so enjoy the festivities. You have already disrupted the party more than enough.'

She had hoped to make a calm exit, but she should have known her mother would never make things that easy for her. Her mother's eyes hardened pointedly in a way she knew all too well.

'Disrupted?' Goldie raised her voice. Both perfectly plucked brows rose in astonishment. 'I'm hardly a wayward child. I just wanted to see my daughter—is that such a bad thing?'

Nicole felt her control snap. 'It's been more than a year since we last spoke. You've never even met your own granddaughter.'

Her mother grasped her hand painfully to stop her from walking away, her eyes filling with tears. 'You're right, darling, I've been awful. But you need to understand—you wouldn't listen to me.'

Nicole grabbed her hand back, massaging her wrist where her mother's nails had dug in.

'You were angry that I wouldn't sell my story to the press. Nothing more and nothing less.'

'I was *worried* about you! I couldn't have my only daughter throwing away her future. Planning to raise that child alone when you could have lived in luxury.' She shook her head. 'But thankfully that argument is null and void now...'

Her mother took a deep breath, a bright smile breaking across her ageing features.

'Just look at you. My Nicole—engaged to a billionaire, living in his penthouse...I'm glad to see you didn't let your silly principles get in the way of common sense.'

Nicole felt nauseated at the look of approval on her mother's face. 'Are you trying to say that I *wanted* this?'

'Of course you didn't.' Goldie laughed. 'Not openly. You're proud, just like your father was—God rest his soul. You're just lucky you have me looking out for you, making it easier for you to do the sensible thing.'

Nicole looked at her mother's smile, feeling a ball of cold dread sink to the pit of her stomach as it all clicked into place. She had been so blind, not wanting to believe her mother could be capable of something so cold. But no one else knew who Anna's father was.

Goldie continued, unaware of any problem. 'You are a mother now—you know what it is to only want the best for your daughter.' She nabbed a flute of champagne from a nearby tray, downing it in one go. 'There's no need to thank me for my efforts. Lord knows I never thought the fool would *propose*, of all things, so I can't take credit for that. All I ask is that you hold on to him now that you've got your claws in.'

She winked, and that one gesture sent Nicole over the edge.

'It was *you*.' Her voice sounded hollow and shrill in her ears. 'You gave that interview, didn't you?'

'Don't worry, it was anonymous—not a soul will ever know.'

'*I* will know!' She forced the words out, the emotion building in her throat. 'How *could* you?'

'Don't act as if I'm the villain here.' Goldie wagged a finger in Nicole's face. 'We both know I've done you a favour. I mean, what else could you do with your career history but marry for money? It's like our little family business.' She laughed weakly, stopping when Nicole's expression darkened. 'All I wanted was a normal life for my daughter...'

Nicole swallowed hard. It was futile to try to explain the concept of normality to her mother—a woman who had strived for superstardom from the moment she'd left home to be a model at sixteen. It was always going to be about what Goldie wanted. Nothing else mattered. She couldn't deal with her mother's narcissistic logic right now.

Her mother's smile changed swiftly and Nicole became aware of a warm, muscular hand settling on her hip. A scent that she had rapidly come to identify as his enveloped her, wrapping her in its warmth. She avoided his eyes, finding herself suddenly unable to look at him for fear he might somehow see her shame. Rigo already believed the worst of her, and once he found out that her mother had been the catalyst behind this whole mess he would never believe that she'd had no involvement.

'Mrs Duvalle, I'm delighted to make your acquaintance.' Rigo smiled, taking Goldie's hand briefly.

Nicole was almost sick at the look of blatant female appreciation on her mother's face as she allowed her red-painted fingernails to rest briefly on Rigo's forearm.

'Soon to be *Miss* Duvalle, I'm afraid.' She blinked once. Twice. A sheen of moisture appeared in her eyes. 'Husband number seven was not so lucky after all. Unless you count his getting lucky with anyone *but* his wife.'

'I'm sorry to hear that.' Rigo's voice was sincere, and his hand still splayed casually across Nicole's hip.

Nicole ignored the sensations his hand threatened to evoke and swallowed past the choking lump now forming in her throat at her mother's words.

So *that* was why her mother had waited until now to out her daughter's story to the tabloids. Her private life had been nothing more than a damned insurance policy for when Goldie's latest marriage went belly-up.

'I'm much more interested in *your* good news.' Goldie touched Rigo's arm once more. 'I had hoped that we might all celebrate together privately…as a family.' She simpered.

That was it for Nicole. She couldn't stand there one more moment and listen to her mother's empty words. She removed Rigo's hand from her side and quickly excused herself, walking towards the nearest doors with as much speed as she could muster. The anger she felt, the pain at her mother's betrayal, it was all too much. She needed to escape.

CHAPTER FIVE

NICOLE WALKED AS far as the elevator bay and exhaled slowly. Seven floors below the ballroom's mezzanine floor she could see hotel staff and guests ambling around the fountain in the lobby. The calm babble of water and the hum of distant voices seemed ridiculously peaceful in comparison to the storm of emotions waging within her.

She would have to tell Rigo. Dishonesty was not a trait that she possessed. It wasn't as if it would come as such a surprise, with what he already knew about her mother anyway. But if she were truly honest with herself she simply didn't want him to know the truth.

She didn't want to tell him that the most pressing reason for her disappearance a year ago had had less to do with him and more to do with her mother, who had even then hoped to use her unborn grandchild for publicity. And, perhaps most embarrassingly of all, that Nicole had chosen to run away rather than stand her ground. Just as she had run away right now.

She watched the progress of an elevator upwards towards her. She didn't even know where she was going, for goodness' sake.

Was she really so weak that she couldn't even be assertive for her own child now? A year ago she had been pregnant and scared. She had turned to Goldie at a time when she'd needed her mother the most, but had been met with nothing but selfishness and greed. 'A baby for a billionaire!' Goldie had practically screamed with delight. And Nicole had instantly known her mistake. She had been a fool ever to think her mother could be relied on for anything other than her own agenda.

She wasn't upset—she had long ago stopped shedding tears over things she couldn't change. She just hated herself for the way she always seemed to let her mother take control of her life. She had played right into Goldie's plan.

She hadn't had to go to Rigo for help, and she certainly hadn't had to accept his proposal.

Maybe she *was* just like her mother.

The thought actually stopped her breathing for a moment. Could that be it? Was she that person who thought the entire world was against her when really she was exactly what they made her out to be?

The elevator arrived with a ping and she hastily stepped inside. The doors began to slide closed, only to be stopped suddenly.

'Where do you think you're going?' Rigo's voice was low, his eyes narrowed in question as he moved his shoulder against the elevator door and effectively blocked her escape.

'I don't know…' Nicole breathed. 'I just needed to get out of there.'

'There was no need to hightail it across the ballroom, drawing everyone's attention.'

Nicole groaned inwardly. Of course everyone would have noticed. They were probably all speculating on what the latest drama was. She leaned her head back against the solid marble wall of the elevator. Steeling herself for what she knew had to come next.

'Nicole…?' he said, his voice demanding an answer.

'I can't marry you.' She forced herself to look him in the eyes as his gaze darkened. 'I can't go ahead with this wedding.'

He was completely silent, allowing his gaze to sweep over her features momentarily before he stepped forward into the lift and let the doors swing shut behind him.

She straightened up to her full height, feeling cornered. 'I'm serious, Rigo.'

'I heard you.' He reached behind her to the panel of lights on the wall, tapping a button at the very top. A voice came from the speaker and Rigo replied in fluent French, looking briefly up at the security camera in the corner. The lift shuddered to life and began moving steadily upwards.

'Where are we going?' Nicole asked, holding on to the railing as they continued to rise higher and higher towards the top of the hotel.

'Somewhere we can talk alone.'

The elevator doors slid open, revealing a corridor with three separate double doors with gold plaques bearing the names of past French presidents.

Nicole followed closely behind Rigo, her feet aching in her high heels, as he led her through the first door. The suite inside was enormous, with stylish dove-grey walls and vaulted ceilings. The antique mahogany furniture looked decades old, with clawed feet and polished silver fittings.

'Do they normally allow you to use the most expensive suite in the hotel for private discussions?'

'They let me do whatever I want.' Rigo shrugged.

'I'd say that kind of freedom is nice.' She bit her lip, feeling the emotions of the past few days threaten to catch up with her.

'We're alone now. So talk.'

Rigo leaned against the side of a dining table, watching her with an intensity that made her insides quake. Where did she even begin to tell him what was going on in her mind right now? All she knew was that her entire being was telling her to run as fast as she could—away from this hotel, their ridiculous plan. Him.

She pressed a hand to her chest, turning away from his scrutiny in the pretence of exploring the suite further. She ran her hand along the ornate back of one of the chairs—another antique, by the looks of it.

The dining table had to be at least ten feet long, she mused. And the room ended in a wall of floor-to-ceiling French windows that led out onto the most spectacular terraced garden. She turned the handle, feeling the cold night air fill her lungs. She could finally take a breath and not feel as if she was drowning.

As she moved out onto the terrace she heard him follow behind her. He wasn't talking, and for that she supposed she should be thankful. She needed to relax if she had any hope of going back to the party. Of course she would go back. She wasn't so cruel as to embarrass him by jilting him in public the way he had rejected her.

The distant memory of him laughing at her in that nightclub threatened the edges of her consciousness. But she didn't believe in giving an eye for an eye, no matter the extent of someone's misdeeds.

'This view is breathtaking.'

She cleared her mind, leaning against the stone wall to peer down at the rooftops of Paris far below. It was like another world up here—so quiet and peaceful. She could stay here forever, just counting the lights on the horizon. If she moved forward just an inch she would be able to see the street where Rigo's apartment was. She tilted her hips, leaning forward just a little more.

Warm, muscular hands settled on her shoulders, pulling her back from the ledge. She could feel Rigo's breath behind her, warm against her bare skin.

'I can admire the view from a distance, but I draw the line at leaning over the edge.'

His voice was like dark chocolate on her frayed senses. His hands still pressed against her bare skin.

'I was just looking.' Her voice came out huskier than she'd intended.

'It's funny, I keep telling myself the same thing.' He moved one fingertip up her arm, tracing her collarbone lightly. 'But then I keep doing this whenever I get the chance.'

Nicole swallowed hard at the sensation his hands on her bare skin evoked. Her shoulders felt tingly and loose, and the feeling was moving steadily downwards. If one touch could make her feel like this, she wondered what his lips might feel like. The thought surprised her, making her angry at herself, angry at him for starting this.

She turned around.

He took a step closer, his hand dropping back to his side. 'I'd imagine you're used to men acting like fools around you.' His mouth turned down at the corners.

Nicole laughed nervously at the ridiculousness of that statement, pushing a tendril of hair behind her ear. 'Last year in Paris was a first for me. With you.'

He had no idea just how telling that statement was. It *had* been a first. He had been *the* first. Not that she would ever fully admit that to him.

Rigo smiled. 'You're good at telling me what I want to hear.'

She tried not to let her wounds show as he took one single step, bringing the heat of his chest almost flush against hers. What was he doing? Her hands reached up to his shoulders, intending to push him away. He was like a wall of hot steel, moulded against her. She could feel the sheer power of him through his suit jacket, barely contained. She arched her head back, knowing she was inviting more but not managing to care. His head lowered, his lips touching the delicate skin beneath her ear. Nicole shivered, arching her neck to give him better access. He kissed a trail of fire down her neck and along her bare shoulder.

'I've been fantasising about this since I saw you tonight,' he whispered against her ear, nipping the skin lightly. 'Probably long before.'

She wished he would stop talking so that she could give in to this completely. She suddenly wanted nothing more than for him to lay her down on a bed so that she could jump into this delicious fire completely and forget about everything else.

But she wouldn't do that. Still, she knew she wouldn't have an excuse to touch him again after tonight. If this was to be goodbye, then she was going to make it count.

She leaned forward, closing the gap between them, and pressed her lips to his. Her kiss was soft…curious, even. His hands captured her hips, pulling her close against him. She could feel every hard plane of his body through the thin lace of her dress as he held her trapped in the circle of his arms.

She wasn't sure when he began to take control of the kiss, but by the time she realised it he had already gained full steam.

She followed his lead, their tongues moving against each other in a steady rhythm. They feasted on each other for so long she almost forgot to breathe, vaguely aware of him guiding her towards the wall behind them, pushing her back flat against it.

His hands cupped her bottom through the lace of her dress as he continued to take possession. She gave as good as she got, holding the front of his shirt in her grip and nipping his lower lip with her teeth. This was fast heading out of her control, but she didn't have the will or the inclination to stop. It felt much too good to walk away just yet. She wanted to see if the reality of him matched up to the memories she had of their night together. It was like stepping back into a dream. She had kissed him first that night, too.

That thought stopped her.

Nicole broke away, pressing her hands against his chest. This was just as bad an idea now as it had been the first time. She wasn't going to make the same mistake twice. She moved away from him, stepping back to the balcony ledge as if the distance might somehow dampen the smouldering heat she could still see blazing in his eyes.

Rigo smiled at her, but it wasn't a smile at all. There was no hint of playfulness in his gaze.

'This isn't a game, Nicole.' He leaned back against the wall, watching her. 'I won't be used as a distraction for whatever is going on in that head of yours.'

'I'll take the blame for that one...' she breathed, straightening the material of her dress and holding her arms around herself in the sudden cold breeze.

She remembered the reason they had come up here in the first place—the conversation with her mother. She felt adrift once again.

'So you were saying you're not going to marry me?' he said coldly.

Nicole bit her lip at his abruptness. 'I can't. Not now that I know...' She shook her head, a shiver running down her bare arms. The temperature was certainly a few degrees lower at this height, but that was only half the reason she felt so cold.

Rigo sighed, shrugging off his jacket in one smooth movement and offering it to her without a word. She accepted it gratefully, draping it around her shoulders and instantly regretting the decision. The material was still warm from his body heat, and it smelled so divine it made her head spin. It was a sin to smell this good... It did funny things to her insides.

'Are you upset about your mother's arrival?' he asked. 'Or is this still about the paparazzi's questions?'

'Just leave it,' she pleaded, feeling cold dread pool in her stomach at the memory of what her mother had revealed. 'It's none of your concern.'

'It is, actually. I can't risk you snapping at photographers when we're trying to build an image together. No matter what they say to provoke you.'

'I wish I *had* snapped, Rigo.' She shook her head. 'All I did was try to stand up for myself for once. And in the end I walked away.'

'In my experience, silence is sometimes the safest option.'

'Maybe I'm tired of being quiet. Maybe I'm *over* having my options taken away from me.'

She thought of her mother's manipulation, cold shame pooling in her veins. They were so different. He had been raised to value his privacy and had always chosen when to disclose his affairs. From the moment she'd been born her mother had used her to promote her own publicity. She had done her first photo shoot when she was four days old, her first solo interview at the age of three. She had been raised at the end of a camera lens.

'Is that actually what you think this marriage is?' His voice hardened. 'Nobody backed you into a corner, Nicole.'

'I cared too much about the implications. I thought I was making the right choice.'

'You cared *too much*?' He laughed—a cruel sound. 'If I had known I was agreeing to marry a martyr perhaps I would have chosen another option.'

Nicole fought against the stinging emotion in her throat. His words were a cruel reminder that this entire relationship was nothing more than a sham. There was no way he could know how much she truly cared. Not just about her daughter, or about what the media said about them, but about what he thought of her, too.

It was ridiculous. After all the times he had hurt her in the short time they'd known one another he still had a strange hold over her emotions. From the moment they'd met she had felt it—that need for him to see her for who she really was. And for a few short hours she had honestly thought he had. But then, as always, reality had come crashing in and he had looked at her with the same scorn that everyone else heaped upon her.

She should just reveal her mother's deception right now. It wouldn't change his opinion of her anyway. No matter how hard she tried to step away from her past it was never going to be enough.

She stepped away from him, bracing her hands on the cold stone balustrade that overlooked the entire city. A tear fell to her cheek and she hastily brushed it away. She wouldn't let him see how deeply his words cut.

Rigo watched Nicole visibly shrink from his words. Even with her back to him he could tell she was hurt. That had not been his intention. He simply didn't understand how a woman who had spent most of her life basking in the limelight of the media could suddenly be so affected by their intrusion.

He laid a hand on her wrist, turning her

to face him and noticing the telltale redness in her eyes.

'I have upset you.' He frowned. 'I'm just trying to say that you always have a choice, Nicole. You *choose* to care. You choose to value everyone else's opinion of you more than your own.' He spoke softly, lifting her chin so that she would look at him.

'Their opinions have always had to matter more,' she whispered. 'It's hard to form a high opinion of yourself when you barely even know who you are.' She stepped away from him, hiding her tears from him once more. 'I've played a part for so long, it just became natural to let others dictate who I should be.'

'What are you talking about?'

'I'm talking about *me*, Rigo.' She sighed. 'How could you want to marry me when you have no idea who I am?'

'I know enough,' he said coldly.

'That's just it. You *think* you know enough but really you know nothing at all.' She shook her head. 'Rigo, I've been a walking sham for most of my life. A persona created by my mother and her publicist,' she continued, refusing to look at him while she spoke.

'I've never broken out of rehab, or slept with married politicians, or done half of what the crazy rumours out there say I have. I was publicly provocative, but once the cameras were gone…I could never follow through. I could never trust anyone enough.'

She looked up at him, meeting his eyes for the first time since their kiss.

'Until that night with you I had never even…I don't know why I'm telling you this.'

Rigo let a harsh breath escape his lungs. 'You had never even *what*, Nicole?' He watched as she visibly tensed at his words. He didn't care if he was being cold. What she was saying was so absurdly far from what he knew about her he found it impossible to believe.

'You were the first man I actually slept with.' She shrugged self-consciously. 'The others were all lies and scandals, drummed up for publicity.'

'Excuse me if I find that hard to believe. You were hardly innocent that night.'

She bit her lip. 'I almost told you—just before we got to your apartment. But then you were saying such wonderful things I just lost my nerve. I was selfish. I worried that it might make you stop, and I didn't want you to see me differently just because of one small detail.'

'That "detail" being your supposed virginity,' Rigo said coldly.

His memory of their night together surfaced painfully. She *had* been nervous. The revelation of what she was telling him now made his stomach clench. Her unashamed response to their lovemaking that night had driven him wild...the way she had been so amazed by her own pleasure. He had been surprised at her shyness about her body, her seemingly unpractised explorations of his body. But once he had found out who she was he had assumed it had all been just a part of her act.

'You're telling me that you were a *virgin*?' he said incredulously, his voice harsher than he'd intended.

'Don't say it like that.' Nicole tugged her wrist out of his grasp, walking away from him into the dim light of the suite's dining room.

'*Dannazione*, Nicole,' he gritted, stepping inside and shutting the door hard behind him.

She turned around, eyes wide at his sudden display of anger.

'Don't just walk away from me after all that.'

'"All that" is my life, Rigo. My truth. I'm not trying to make you feel guilty, or gain sympathy. I just needed to talk about something real for once!' she exclaimed. 'Do you know what? Let's just forget this conversation ever happened and you can go back to whatever you thought of me before. Whatever makes you feel better.'

'You honestly think I could *forget* knowing that I took your virginity and then threw you out on the street?' Agitated, he ran a hand through his hair. 'You walked away that morning after I practically called you a whore. Then, even when you knew that the child you carried was mine, you walked away again.'

'Oh, no. You don't get to turn this around on *me* just because you've realised how callous you actually are. I walked up to you in the middle of a crowded nightclub, Rigo, because you refused to answer any of my calls. I was honest about my pregnancy. The only reason I chose not to push any harder was because you made it brutally clear what you thought of me—and of the child I carried.'

Her words were like cold water over his temper. He had been abrupt and forbidding, refusing to entertain her from the moment she had shown up unannounced at his favourite club. The thought suddenly filled him with cold shame.

'You *laughed* at me, Rigo. You humiliated me in front of all your rich, sophisticated friends. It's probably best that this sham doesn't go ahead, because I don't think I could survive being married to a man I know doesn't respect me.'

'Nicole...' He shook his head, needing her to stop talking so that he could process the reshuffling of the facts in his mind.

'I need to leave, Rigo. Please don't follow me.'

He caught a glimpse of the tears in her eyes for a split second before she turned and walked away, disappearing through the suite in a blur of long legs and pale blue silk.

With every passing second he felt his temper ebb and the cold realisation of his own actions set in. He had made presumptions about her character from the moment they'd met, just as she had accused him of doing. But was it entirely his fault when she had worked tirelessly to make the media believe she was someone else?

He thought of the woman he had bedded that night, of her hushed moans and the momentary cry of pain that he had presumed was some sort of theatrical move. He had been so blind, and he had coldly brushed the intense feelings from their lovemaking aside once he'd learned her name the next morning.

He had rushed things. He hadn't known her from the English tabloids so he had powered ahead, giving in to the ridiculous heat that had burned between them. He knew that his reaction on finding out who she was had been exaggerated. But after being fooled by a woman once before on such an enormous, soul-wrenching scale, his pride wasn't something he took lightly. He had called her a gold-digging whore. And then he had humiliated her.

The memory sat heavily in his gut.

This arrangement was proving more complicated than he had ever imagined. The waters had grown murky and he didn't like it one bit. He would have to find a way to make peace with his wife-to-be or this marriage was never going to work.

Nicole sat cross-legged in the middle of the nursery. Anna's chubby legs kicked hard in the air as she tried to roll over on the carpet. It was already midmorning and there had been no sign of Rigo coming home since last night. She tried to focus on folding Anna's belongings into her small case, hoping it might calm the storm of emotions going through her brain. She hadn't planned on letting things get so personal last night. And she hadn't meant that kiss.

What on earth had been going through her head to let Rigo know that she had been a virgin? It didn't really make a difference to their situation. It had been her own private secret, along with the memories she held close of the one night when she had trusted a man enough to completely let go and take her own pleasure. She didn't know why she had waited so long, but there it was. And now the look of horror on his face would ruin that memory for her forever.

Anna squealed, looking at a spot directly

behind her. Nicole knew she would find Rigo standing at the door even before she smelled his cologne on the air. His hair was wet, as though he had just stepped out of the shower. His blue eyes were darker than usual—or was it the faint shadows under his eyes that made them seem so? Either way, he looked both terrible and devastatingly handsome at the same time. It was quite an accomplishment.

He was silent for a moment, his gaze trained on Anna as she continued to try to roll onto her stomach, laughing as she fell back each time. 'The housekeeper told me that you were packing,' he said finally.

'I asked her to help but she said she had to clear it with you first.' Nicole sighed. 'Thankfully I am under no such obligation.'

'Can we at least talk before you go barrelling out of here?' he said darkly. 'Do you even know where you will go?'

Nicole steeled her resolve. He knew that she had very few options here. But her pride wouldn't let her stay a moment longer.

She stood up, facing him with her chin held high. 'I won't talk to the press. You can pretend the engagement still stands if you want. We can keep this quiet for as long as you need for your deal to go through. Pretend the wedding has been postponed or something.'

'What can I do to make you stay?' He stood absolutely still, his hands deep in his pockets as he held her gaze.

Nicole shook her head, looking away from him and trying to find the right combination of words to let him know she couldn't do this any more.

Rigo's phone sounded, startling Anna with its shrillness. The baby began to sob. Nicole bent down to scoop her up in her arms, holding her close as Rigo began having what sounded like quite an urgent conversation in Italian.

He ended the call, looking up at her with the closest thing to panic as she had ever seen on his face. 'Alberto has just called to say that the magazine team is on its way up in the lift.'

'The interview… It's today?' Nicole felt her heart beating hard in her chest.

She had been gearing up for this all week. They were to present the world with an intimate portrait of them in their home to go along with the photographs of their engagement party. The prep work had been done with the PR team, and her pre-approved outfit hung pressed and waiting in the dressing room. It was a vital piece of this facade to set the scandal straight and get the media on their side.

'I've had my phone turned off since last night.' He pinched the bridge of his nose hard. 'Nicole, I know that I have no right to ask you for help but… I need you by my side.'

Nicole bit her lip. *I need you.* She must be mad, but she didn't want to let him down. She nodded, watching his shoulders sag with relief.

The magazine that would cover their entire sensational love story had competed against countless others to win the contract. In the end it had all come down to privacy for Rigo. He wanted a respectable British publication to take charge of the coverage, with the money raised from the deal going straight into his parents' charity.

The team was busy setting up lighting around the seating area. Nicole sat by his side, dressed in jeans and a soft pink top that cut across her collarbone to sit at the tops of her shoulders. She looked deceptively relaxed in the soft morning light.

While they waited Anna sat propped on her lap in pink baby pyjamas, all ready for her afternoon nap.

The make-up artist came over, with her belt filled with brushes. 'I just want to touch up a few bits, Miss Duvalle, if that's okay?' She gestured to a stool set up across the room.

Nicole looked at him for a moment, her expression strange. 'Would you…hold her?' she asked quietly, looking up briefly to where the journalist sat near them, taking notes and preparing for their interview. Anna might not be featuring in the photo shoot—both Nicole and Rigo had been clear about that—but even behind the scenes they were on show.

Rigo cleared his throat, nodding as casually as he could before accepting the pink bundle into his arms. He probably wasn't holding her correctly, he thought suddenly. He looked to Nicole, but she was already sitting on the stool with her eyes closed as the make-up woman deftly swept a brush over her cheeks.

He looked back down at the child. She sat

facing away from him, looking towards the window. He hadn't been around babies much in his lifetime—not at all, really. She shifted her weight, almost jumping off his lap as a bird flew down to land on the balcony outside. Her excitement was instantaneous, and her features lit up with glee as she pointed one chubby finger towards the creature.

Rigo smiled. He couldn't help it. Her laughter was infectious, just like her mother's.

He stood up, walking closer to the window and holding her tight against his chest. She sat relaxed in his arms, her attention entirely focused on the creature pecking at the moss on the balcony ledge.

A bright flash drowned them both in sudden blinding light. Anna's tiny features scrunched up with surprise before she let out a piercing wail. The cameraman stood guiltily a few feet away. Rigo felt the sudden urge to punch the man full force in the face. He controlled himself, not shouting at the oaf for fear of upsetting the baby further.

He looked across the room to Nicole, silently begging her to help. Anna was inconsolable now.

Nicole stood swiftly, crossing the room to

take Anna into her arms. The child was instantly soothed, looking briefly up at him with a mixture of fear and recrimination. He took the chance to retreat, speaking sternly to the cameraman so that they didn't have a repeat incident and making sure he deleted the photo from his camera.

As the director announced that they were all set Nicole handed the child over to the nanny for her nap. The twenty-minute photo session drained them, with all the forced poses and orders to smile on cue. They took a few romantic 'couple' shots before beginning the interview.

Rigo kept his arm slung around Nicole's shoulders on the back of the sofa. They needed to seem at ease with each other, but she was as tense as an ironing board. When he'd leaned over to lay a kiss on her lips at the photographer's suggestion he might as well have kissed a block of ice.

'So let's start with what exactly are the boundaries for the big day?'

The female journalist's husky Scottish accent interrupted the tense silence in the aftermath of the disastrous photo shoot. She placed a digital recorder on the futon between them, its red light blinking.

Rigo spoke, his answers all pre-rehearsed. 'We expect discretion at all times, with only a prearranged time slot for photographs.'

The woman nodded, ticking a box on her list. 'Will we be allowed access to the bride as she prepares? We would love to get some candid shots of all aspects of the day.'

'No,' Nicole said suddenly. 'I mean…I don't think I would be comfortable with that.'

Rigo looked at her pointedly, laying his hand gently on her thigh. 'What my beautiful fiancée means to say is that she'll likely be too nervous for that on the day.'

The journalist narrowed her eyes, clearly unimpressed at the answer. She flipped through some of the photographs from the engagement party the night before, pausing on one.

She looked up, a gleam appearing in her eyes. 'Your mother wasn't invited to the party last night, Nicole?' she asked in her simpering voice. 'Why was that?'

'She was invited. There was simply a mix-up with the list,' Rigo said quickly.

'And yet these photos clearly show Nicole

and Goldie having what looks like a heated argument.' She raised her brow.

Rigo looked to Nicole, noticing the sudden look of horror on her face. She masked it quickly, taking a sip from her glass of lemon water.

'There was no argument, Diane. Move on, please,' she said harshly.

Rigo frowned at Nicole's use of the woman's first name. He had noticed the immediate tensing in Nicole when they had been introduced to the woman who would write their article, but he had put it down to nerves. Now, looking at the two women staring each other down, he wasn't so sure.

'From what I hear, you should be *thanking* your mother. Not arguing with her.' The woman continued to pout in that same ridiculous way, staring at Nicole like an eagle watching her prey.

'You're here to ask questions about the wedding. Do your damned job,' Nicole said quickly, before moving a hand to her mouth with instant regret.

Rigo sat forward, pressing a button on the digital recorder swiftly. 'I think we need to take a break.' He stood, gesturing for Nicole to follow him.

The woman—Diane—spoke quickly. 'Oh, no, I *am* here to do my job after all. So as a matter of interest for the article, does your fiancé know the kind of family he's marrying into?'

'Diane…' Nicole shook her head sadly, a bleak look in her eyes.

'This is not proper conduct when in the home of your subjects.' Rigo walked towards Diane, using his height to appear imposing towards the woman.

'I just thought that you might want to know a few things about your wonderful bride-to-be. Like the fact that she and her mother are the most slippery creatures to walk this planet.'

'You have personal experience with my fiancée that gives you this opinion?' Rigo asked.

Diane spluttered at his challenge. 'Her mother is a witch, a horrible—'

'Goldie Duvalle is not in this room, and I would like to know why you are attacking her daughter—unless you have some personal reason.'

The woman froze, her mouth opening and closing twice in quick succession.

'That's what I thought.' Rigo shook his head, looking down at his designer watch. 'I don't have any more time for this. Leave now. All of you. You've got what you came for.'

Nicole sat completely still, with her shoulders down so far he thought she might be trying to disappear into the settee. As the magazine crew packed up their things and filed out into the hall, the interviewer looked pointedly at Nicole one last time.

'Oh, and, Diane, was it?' Rigo said darkly. 'I'd expect a call from your superiors this afternoon if I were you. You'll want to start job-hunting.'

'You people think you run the world!' she said angrily as Rigo herded her out through the door. He closed it with a resounding snap as she continued to curse him from the other side.

Rigo looked down at his fiancée, his gut tightening as he noticed her pale face. He refilled her glass of lemon water, offering it to her.

She took a sip, looking away from him towards the windows. 'I didn't know it would be her doing the interview.'

'I take it from that display of hostility that you are previously acquainted?'

'Yes. You could say that.' Nicole shook her head sadly. 'The man my mother is currently getting a divorce from is Diane's seventy-year-old father.'

CHAPTER SIX

NICOLE FELT THE tension in her temples rise to breaking point. 'That's the third time she has confronted me like that and I still never know what to say to her.'

'Why would you say anything at all?' Rigo shrugged. 'She is clearly angry at your mother and using you as a scapegoat.'

'I sympathise with her. I feel guilty about what my mother did to her family. Her parents had been happily married for decades before…' She felt sadness encompass her, knowing exactly what it felt like to have your parents disappoint you that way. 'My mother has this uncanny knack for taking someone's life and turning it completely upside down.'

She had been sure that Diane knew about her mother giving that interview, had braced herself for the other woman to announce it and ruin the shaky friendship that she and Rigo seemed to have come to. But now she was gone, and they were standing here discussing her mother. She knew the time had come to tell him.

'You are not your mother's keeper, Nicole. Do you realise that?' Rigo said softly. 'She is a grown woman who is responsible for her own actions.'

'Most of the time her actions directly affect me in some way or another.' Nicole cleared her throat, looking up at him. 'Diane was right. I *was* arguing with her last night.'

'That's why you ran out?'

She nodded, swallowing the lump in her throat. 'She told me something so awful that I just couldn't bear to stand across from her a moment longer.' She stepped away from him, taking a deep breath as she tried to find the right words. Wringing her hands, she turned back to face him. 'Goldie was the anonymous source, Rigo. She's the one who leaked the story.'

He was completely silent for a moment, looking at her with something akin to curiosity. 'Why didn't you tell me this last night, when you were confessing all your sins?'

'I was afraid of how you might react.'

'In other words, you thought I would believe you had a part in it?'

Nicole paused, her eyelids fluttering up to meet his gaze. 'Well, don't you?'

Rigo shook his head, shoving his hands deep into his pockets. 'Before last night, maybe. But I'm coming to see that I've been very quick to judge you.'

'Well, I suppose I should be thankful for that, at least.'

'Nicole, I can see why you want to walk away from this marriage now. But I'm asking you to reconsider. For Anna, if nothing else.'

'We proved to each other last night that we can't be civil or separate in this arrangement. We're just not good for each other,' she said quietly.

He was quiet for a moment, looking out the window. 'Nicole, I want this marriage to work. If that means me staying as far away as possible then I will do it. To keep you and Anna safe.'

She looked into his eyes. He was being earnest. But she didn't want him to stay away at all—that was the problem. She walked away from him, crossing her arms over her chest as she followed the progress of one errant raindrop down the window. Within a matter of seconds it had begun to pour, the landscape turning a dull grey.

She knew that backing out of their arrangement had been a decision made in the heat of the moment. Marrying Rigo *was* the best choice for Anna and it always would be. Looking into his eyes, she could feel the shift between them—not quite enemies any longer, but it had put them in a kind of limbo. He made her feel off balance…as if simply being around him for too long put her at risk of making a fool of herself all over again.

'Send the staff away,' she said suddenly. 'Just until we leave for the wedding. Give them extended holiday leave. Then there will be no need for us to share a bed. We can each have our space until the wedding is over.'

'Consider it done.' Rigo nodded once, his face completely unreadable.

'Thank you.' Nicole took a deep breath, feeling decidedly less filled with dread than she had this morning. And yet she still felt that same tug of unease in the back of her mind. As if somehow by putting more distance between them she was denying herself something vital. But she didn't need Rigo's kisses in her life, and she definitely didn't need him in her bed. Sleeping or otherwise. Boundaries were the only thing protecting her from the damage this man could do to her if she ever let him close again. This was safe.

Nicole looked down at the slim diamond-encrusted watch on her wrist and felt her anxiety peak. The rehearsal dinner was due to start in twenty minutes and Rigo hadn't arrived yet. His entire family was downstairs, waiting to meet his bride-to-be for the first time, and she couldn't hide up here a moment longer.

She hadn't seen him for more than a passing greeting in the past weeks, since the magazine debacle. True to his word, he'd had Diane fired and a new journalist had taken her place. The interview had gone without a hitch and now the whole world was geared up and waiting with bated breath to witness the wedding of the decade.

She took in her reflection in the mirror, frowning at the lines between her brows. Her mother had always told her that frowning and laughing too much was a recipe for crow's feet. She shrugged off the thought. Her mother was the last person she needed to be thinking of right now. She was probably down there already, guzzling champagne and on the lookout for husband number eight.

As expected, the PR team had advised that Goldie should not be kept out of the celebrations, to avoid any negative speculation. Well, that was their official standpoint, but Nicole had a feeling that Rigo didn't want her mother tempted to do any more anonymous interviews before his Fournier deal was put through. The last thing they needed was more scandal.

The secret location for their wedding had been leaked in the past week, but Rigo had assured her that an increased security presence would deter any would-be paparazzi gatecrashers. Truth be told, it didn't worry her too much. Anna was staying put in Paris until Nicole returned to collect her for their honeymoon.

Forty-eight hours apart seemed like a lifetime right now, but she knew she had done the right thing. Rigo had told her his parents were waiting impatiently to meet their first grandchild, having just returned from the Indian Ocean that morning. He hadn't spoken of his father much, but she'd got the impression that his family dynamic was one of ease. She just hoped that she gave a better impression to them than she had given to his brother on their first meeting.

Nicole walked down the sweeping staircase, taking in the throng of guests in the chateau's large reception area. She stood alone at the bottom, looking around for a familiar face and cursing her fiancé. She recognised some of the faces from their engagement party, but without Rigo to smooth the way she felt small and insignificant. Technically, she was the hostess—she should be commanding the event. And yet she wanted nothing more than to run back up the stairs and hide.

A man stood in the centre of the gathering, his presence seeming to make the guests flock around him. His resemblance to her future husband was remarkable—the only difference being the mop of grey waves that crowned his head and his slightly age-weathered features. A small, elegantly dressed woman stood by his side. Valerio Marchesi stepped close to the woman and smiled, dropping a familiar kiss on her cheek before she took him into a warm embrace.

Nicole forced herself to walk the few steps across the room, noting Rigo's brother tense as he spotted her.

'I wonder if my brother has decided to bolt,' he said wryly, looking down at her with moderate disapproval. 'It would be an awful pity to leave you jilted, Nicole.'

The older brunette stepped forward, taking her in from head to toe. 'You must be my future daughter-in-law,' she said, her voice heavily accented. 'I must apologise that you're being left to introduce yourself alone. I can imagine this is quite intimidating.'

'Rigo has likely been delayed at the office,' she said, her voice shaking slightly with nerves. 'But I'm sure he'll be here soon.'

Rigo's mother made no move to embrace her nor did she formally introduce herself. His father was deep in conversation and made no move to greet her. Nicole stood in awkward silence, not quite knowing what move to make next.

Her relief when the main door opened was palpable, and the small gathering turned as

Rigo entered. He was commandeered instantly by a group of friends near the doorway.

'My son likes to make an entrance.' A deep male voice boomed next to her. 'My apologies for not greeting you straight away. These buffoons still think I hold some power in the fashion industry.' The man chuckled, the scent of red wine on his breath as he leaned forward. 'I'm Amerigo Marchesi Senior. You've met my wife, Renata?'

He embraced Nicole with the force of a bear, dropping a warm kiss on each cheek before motioning for his wife to do the same.

Nicole noted the tightness around Rigo's mother's mouth as she leaned forward to embrace her. She got the distinct impression that the woman already disliked her. Wonderful.

'We are quite eager to meet little Anna, aren't we, *tesoro*?' Amerigo smiled.

Renata raised a brow, unimpressed. 'Rigo has been very tight-lipped about it all. We were only told this week, as a matter of fact. Our only grandchild and we haven't even seen a photograph.' Renata pursed her lips, looking across to where her son stood.

Nicole saw a telltale tremor in Renata's lower lip for a brief moment before the woman covered it up by taking a sip from her wine glass. She was hurt at being kept out of the loop. Nicole felt a pang of sympathy for the woman.

She opened her purse, taking out the photograph of Anna that she carried with her for good luck. She held the glossy image out to the older woman, noting how her eyes softened as she accepted it and cradled it in her hands.

'She has the Marchesi eyes,' she whispered with awe. 'I can hardly believe that she is real—she looks like a little doll.'

'She is very like Rigo,' Nicole agreed, missing her daughter intensely.

'Ah, but she has hair like her mother.' Amerigo smiled, taking her hand in his own. 'You will make a beautiful bride, Nicole. And I wish you both great happiness.'

Nicole felt her throat tighten at the man's words. He was nothing like she had imagined. Neither of them were. She shook her head as Renata made to return the picture. 'No, please keep it. I have plenty more.'

As Amerigo moved away to go and greet his son Renata took her hand, gesturing for them to move to the side of the room together. Nicole waited for the disapproval, the scorn that she expected as the woman who had brought scandal on this ancient family. She was completely taken by surprise when Renata leaned forward and hugged her—a real embrace, unlike the formal one before. She relaxed her shoulders, feeling the warmth seep into her bones.

The older woman pulled back a fraction. 'I'm sorry if I'm giving you mixed signals, my dear. But I wasn't sure…'

What she had been about to say was drowned out by a familiar high-pitched voice. Nicole's mother was making her way towards them across the hall. 'I simply *must* introduce myself to the mother of the groom.' Goldie fawned over Renata, laying an exaggerated kiss on each of her cheeks. 'Isn't this all just so heartbreakingly romantic?'

'Yes, I suppose so,' Renata said demurely, taking a discreet look down at the photograph in her hand and smiling. 'I'm looking forward to having them both in Tuscany once this has all died down. I can't wait to get my hands on this little *piccolina*.'

Nicole saw the light die in Goldie's eyes

as they narrowed in on the photograph. 'Oh, how *delightful*. May I see?'

Before Nicole could intervene, Goldie had reached out and grabbed it from Renata's hands.

'*So* nice of you to make plans with the grandparents, Nicole.' Goldie's lips pursed as she stared at Anna's picture. 'I'm not privileged enough to meet the little princess, you see,' she said darkly.

'Mum, why don't we go outside?' Nicole stepped forward, taking hold of her mother's elbow gently.

Goldie shrugged her off. 'I thought she'd have nice tanned skin, like her father,' she mused, looking closely at the picture. 'Thank goodness she didn't get his nose, though.'

'I'll take that back, thank you.' Renata reached out and plucked the photograph from Goldie's hands just as Rigo appeared beside them.

'Is everything all right here, ladies?'

'Oh, here he is—the knight in shining armour,' Goldie spat. 'I've just had the privilege of meeting your mother, Signor Marchesi.'

She exaggerated the *r*'s with a roll of her

tongue and Nicole suddenly realised her mother was roaring drunk.

'Mum, perhaps you should go and drink some water,' Nicole suggested weakly, seeing that her mother's mood had shifted for the worse.

'Oh, shut up, Nicole,' Goldie said, pushing her hand away with vehemence. 'Look at you—pretending to be all sweetness and sophistication.' Goldie continued to raise her voice, looking to Renata, who was frozen in shock. '*I'm* the one who did all this for her. *Me!* You'd still be hiding away if I hadn't drawn you out.' She stepped dangerously close to Nicole, the smell of sour champagne heavy on her breath. 'And suddenly you're too good for me? You are nothing but an ungrateful little—'

Rigo caught Goldie's hand just as it flew up into the air. The look of thunder on his face made Nicole's stomach flip. 'That will be enough,' he said darkly.

The entire room full of guests had turned to watch the altercation. Nicole felt hot embarrassment sweep up her neck and into her cheeks. Rigo was fully prepared to deal with Goldie and send her out on her ear—

she could see that clearly. But something in his face prompted her to step forward, placing her hand on her mother's arm.

'I would advise you to leave now if you ever hope to meet your grandchild at all,' she said quietly, knowing Renata was still within earshot.

'You owe me...' Goldie slurred. 'You know what I did—'

'I owe you *nothing*,' Nicole said with cold finality. 'You are lucky that I'm still speaking to you after the way you've treated me. Now please leave before we have to do this the hard way.'

Goldie looked as if she was going to fight, and her eyes narrowed horribly on Rigo's mother. But finally, with a heaving sigh, she shook her head and allowed Rigo to guide her across the hall.

'I'm sorry you had to witness that.' Nicole turned to Renata.

'She is the one who should be sorry, my girl.' Rigo's mother shook her head. 'You shouldn't have to tolerate that kind of intimidation—least of all from your mother.'

'She means well...I think,' Nicole said.

Renata sighed. 'You have a kind heart, Nicole. Take my advice and protect it from people who don't take care with it.'

Nicole smiled, still preoccupied with watching Rigo's progress across the room. It was a strange feeling, knowing she suddenly had someone looking out for her. That he was prepared to stand in her corner and fight. She had grown used to conceding defeat time and time again. The comfort of telling herself that she didn't care had always been like a blanket, stopping her from changing or growing. Somehow knowing that he thought she was worth defending gave her the confidence to want to defend *herself*. She didn't want to be weak anymore. She wanted to care enough about being treated badly that she would stand up and fight her own ground.

'I want to wish my brother and his beautiful bride-to-be a long and happy marriage.' Valerio Marchesi clapped his older brother hard on the back. '*Cent'anni*—to one hundred years!' He shouted the traditional Italian toast, which was quickly repeated by the intimate gathering of guests at the rehearsal dinner.

'*Grazie*, little brother.' Rigo raised his

glass briefly, before downing the champagne in one go.

All his senses were heightened by the presence of the woman by his side. Nicole looked so quietly radiant in her strapless black dress that anyone might think her silence all evening was simply a result of bridal nerves. But he knew better.

He silently cursed Goldie Duvalle for being such a callous, selfish human being. It had taken all his willpower to step back. Nicole had handled the situation with infinitely more grace than he would have. Rehearsal dinner be damned—he'd wanted nothing more than to have the woman dragged out of the room by security and thrown on the first flight back to wherever she'd come from.

He half listened to his father and brother, who were deep in conversation comparing their latest travel stories. Valerio Marchesi was a wild card. He had declined their father's invitation into the family business in order to pursue his own career, chartering yachts and luxury sailing boats around the Caribbean. Now, ten years later, he was a success in his own right, co-owner of one of the biggest luxury maritime-vessel charter companies in the world.

Rigo envied his younger brother his freedom, his lack of responsibility. Normally he would have been eager to hear about Valerio's pirate-like exploits on the high seas, but tonight his mind just wasn't focused. Try as he did to stop them, his eyes kept straying to Nicole.

Once the dinner had ended and all the wine had been drunk, the guests began to filter up to their rooms. He stood in the hallway with his parents to say goodnight. Nicole was deep in conversation with his mother and aunts. Valerio stood by his side, arms crossed, filled with the same tension he had seen in him all evening.

'You look s if you've sucked on a lemon.' Rigo raised a brow at his younger brother. 'Careful, or I might think your speech was insincere.'

'I just can't get my head around your logic, that's all.' Valerio shrugged. 'But just because I don't agree with it, it doesn't mean I don't wish you happiness.'

'If you're worried I haven't learned something in the past ten years, then you can relax. This is nowhere near the same situation,' Rigo warned him, not wanting to get into a conversation about his disastrous relationship history. He knew his family had been affected by his relationship with Lydia, but seeing the tension in his brother's face made it clear that he should have been more considerate in breaking the news this time.

'No, it's not. At least this time you knew the woman was a gold-digger *before* you arranged the wedding.' Valerio looked at him. 'I just don't want to see you go through the same hell you did with Lydia. That she-beast changed you.'

'I learned a valuable lesson from that "she-beast".' Rigo smiled darkly. 'Never trust a woman with anything more than your credit card. And even then at least check the bills.'

His smile died on his lips as he turned to see Nicole standing by his side, a mask of hurt on her face.

Valerio cleared his throat, taking his mother's arm and ushering her up the stairs with a murmured goodnight.

Nicole narrowed her eyes at him, her shoulders squared. 'She-beast?' she said quietly.

'That conversation wasn't about you.' He

forced an easy smile, taking her hand into his. She pushed it away. 'We were talking about someone else.'

She nodded once, not quite seeming to relax. 'Charming. Your brother doesn't like me at all.'

'My not-so-little brother has a very large, very annoying sense of protectiveness towards me.' Rigo sighed, looking up at where Valerio and his mother were just disappearing around the corner at the top of the stairs. 'You're not the only person I've hurt in the past due to my own stubbornness.'

She looked up at him. 'That doesn't explain why he's taking it out on me.'

'It's this situation we're in. This whirlwind wedding. It's an uncomfortable reminder for them all of the last time I told them I was engaged.'

Rigo continued, oblivious to the horrified expression she knew must be on her face. 'I was engaged to be married ten years ago and it ended…badly.'

'What happened?' Nicole asked, even though a part of her didn't want to believe he'd been engaged to someone else at all.

'Just the usual stuff.' He shrugged, looking down at the floor briefly. 'The breakup was rather messy, and my mother took it quite hard. The wedding had been planned, invitations sent out.'

'That sounds like a nightmare,' she breathed.

A strange look came over his face—a mask of emotion so intense it took her breath away. All of a sudden it was gone, replaced by a blank stare.

'It was many years ago, Nicole.'

He reached down to take her hand in his once more and this time she didn't push it away. Knowing he had a heart after all, knowing he had been affected on some level by heartache, made her want to be the one to heal him.

She had felt it all evening—this tingling sensation in her chest that increased as their wedding day grew nearer. She'd kept telling herself that this was just another promotional appearance, that it meant nothing. But meeting his family and presenting them with this show of love and devotion had made her begin to wish it wasn't all an act.

But she knew from experience that hope was a dangerous emotion.

* * *

The next morning Nicole stood in front of the full-length mirror with a sense of over-whelming awe. Her wedding gown truly was a work of art, with the fitted bodice hugging her curves like a second skin before flow-ing out in an elaborate skirt from just above her knee.

It was everything she had never dared to imagine for herself. She turned to the side, taking in the intricate lace beading down her back and the long train of silk and tulle that flowed out behind her. Women should be able to wear gowns like this every day, she thought, smiling to herself. She felt like royalty.

Rigo's mother stepped closer to her side. 'My mother stood with me like this on the morning of my wedding, you know.' Her deep blue eyes were filled with warmth. 'She and her sisters had spent weeks mak-ing my dress, but this veil was her own per-sonal project.'

She held out a length of delicately embroi-dered vintage lace.

'She poured her heart and soul into it, and told me it would bring me and my new husband strong love and strong sons…daughters in your case.' She smiled, brushing away an errant tear. 'I didn't have any daughters of my own, so I'm passing down this gift to you. Don't worry—the stylists know not to cross me.'

'Oh, Renata, that's such a beautiful gesture.' Nicole's hands traced the delicate pattern of hand-sewn embellishments.

'It's my pleasure. And I hope one day you will have the gift of placing this on your own daughter's head when she marries the one she loves.'

Nicole dipped down as her future mother-in-law pinned the delicate veil in place and the stylists began to tease out the loose waves of her hair underneath. The overall effect was so classically stunning she was speechless.

'Love him with all your heart, Nicole. And I'll never have to worry about him again.'

Renata kissed her lightly on each cheek before disappearing out the door.

Nicole frowned at the woman's words, feeling them settle in her chest. His mother believed them to be deeply in love. She was happy for them. If she knew the truth it would probably break her heart.

Nicole took a deep breath and tried to calm her nerves as she was left alone for a few moments in the bridal suite. This was just another day—nothing special, she told herself.

As she made her way down the staircase to meet the events team she became conscious of the fact that she had no bridesmaids and no flower girls to stand with. Only the kind-faced event co-ordinator, who now stood on the steps to escort her outside to the grounds of the chateau, where a beautiful chapel nestled halfway into the forest.

The co-ordinator and her staff hurriedly adjusted her train before the door to the chapel was thrown open. Nicole stood still at the entryway, having chosen not to have anyone walk her down the aisle. She was making her own choices now, so it seemed fitting to give herself away.

As the doors opened and she began to walk slowly down the aisle she was aware of the guests' hushed breaths and sighs of approval.

She held her breath as Rigo turned to face her. The look of silent awe in his eyes almost brought her to a grinding halt. She reminded herself to keep moving towards him, to focus on his face and forget about everything else.

He wore a sleekly cut designer tuxedo, and his brother stood by his side in the same. She was completely on show and yet she didn't feel exposed. She felt confident with his eyes on hers. She felt a sense of anticipation as she got closer and closer to him. But as she came to a stop by his side and looked up at him the enormity of what they were about to commit to was overwhelming.

Rigo's hand enveloped hers as the priest began the ceremony and she fought to focus on the various prayers, then automatically repeated the phrases.

When the moment finally came for her to slide a thick gold band onto Rigo's third finger as a symbol of their eternal devotion, to her embarrassment she felt her fingers shake uncontrollably. His tanned, muscular fingers covered hers and she saw the spark of possession in his eyes as he placed an identical gold band onto her finger.

The priest pronounced them husband and wife.

Nicole felt her breath catch in her throat at the look of dark possession in Rigo's gaze. He took no time in pressing his lips to hers, moving his hand to her waist as he pulled her close. The kiss was a part of the ceremony, she told herself. But as he released his breath slowly she felt his fingers tremble against her waist. That one sign of weakness made her wonder if perhaps she wasn't the only one struggling not to be affected.

He broke the kiss after a respectable amount of time—they were in a church after all—but the heat in his gaze was just for her. She knew with sudden clarity that this moment would be scorched on her memory forever, no matter what came after.

The wedding reception passed in a blur of wine and dancing. By the time Rigo's father swept her up on the dance floor for the third time her feet were aching to escape from their designer shoe prisons.

'May I cut in?'

Rigo's voice came from somewhere behind her left ear as the music slowed down to a steady beat. They had shared a first dance already, earlier in the evening. The memory of it still clung to her skin, where he had pressed his face against her neck.

The photographers had been present then, trying their best to melt into the background but not really succeeding. All day he had touched her and kissed her, their charade successfully convincing the world of their marital bliss. But her traitorous body didn't seem to realise that this wasn't real. That he was playing a part.

Rigo's hands rested low on her waist, his fingertips pressing just above her hips. As he pulled her close she thought she heard him release his breath on a deep sigh. But when she looked up he was looking away from her. She laid her head against his chest, her hands gripping on to the back of his jacket as she breathed in the scent of him.

All too soon the guests had formed a line to wish them well as they made the traditional exit through the arched arms of Rigo's family and friends.

They made their way in silence up the stone steps to the master suite at the top of the chateau. Nicole stopped for a moment in the middle of the corridor to slip her shoes off her feet. She moaned with relief as her aching toes lay flat on the carpeted floor.

'Better?' Rigo said huskily.

She nodded. 'It's a long walk up here. Especially in heels.'

He took a step towards her, cupping her face in one hand. 'I can carry you if you like?'

When she didn't immediately respond he stepped closer again, his mouth lowering to lay another kiss on her neck. 'I haven't been able to stop inhaling this delicious scent all day.'

'The photographers are gone, Rigo,' she breathed, trying to ignore the immediate frisson of arousal that coursed through her body.

'Let's pretend they're not.'

Those words seemed to unlock a tension inside her that she hadn't known was there. This kiss was different from the others— more urgent. His hands cupped her jaw, holding her in place as his tongue moved against hers. Their breath mingled into one as the rest of the world fell away. There was no one watching them now, no one to perform for. This was just for them.

She stopped holding back and gave in to the arousal that threatened to burn her up, grabbing a fistful of his hair and groaning into his mouth as he pressed the evidence of his arousal against her. She wanted him. She wanted everything that she knew he couldn't give her. And yet maybe just having tonight might make whatever came after easier to survive.

It suddenly seemed impossible to stop.

She took a deep breath, their eyes locked in the dim light of the corridor. 'Rigo... If we go into that bedroom together, I want it to be real.'

Rigo took her hand, pressing it to the hard beating of his heart through his shirt. 'Do you actually doubt that it is?'

She bit her lip, holding on to his hand as he led her down the hall and into the honeymoon suite. His lips were on hers as soon as the door had closed behind them. She barely had a moment to appreciate the romantic candlelight that glowed around the room before he was burning her up all over again. And, oh, it was good to burn.

She turned and swept her hair to the side so that he could access the row of tiny pearl closures that ran down to the base of her spine.

Per l'amore di Dio—is this a dress or a straitjacket?' Rigo breathed, popping open the tiny buttons one by one at a torturously slow pace. 'It would be easier to just rip them open.'

'It would. But you won't.' She bit her lip. 'At least I hope you won't.'

'I can tell that you love this dress, so I will try to control myself.'

He continued popping the tiny pearl fastenings until the dress was loose enough for her to shimmy it down. She did love this dress—not because it was haute couture, or because it was miles ahead of the fashion trend. She loved it because *he* loved it. And it would remind her forever of the awestruck look on his face as she'd walked down the aisle to become his wife.

Nicole let the material fall slowly down her body to the floor before stepping out of the mountain of silk and chiffon. With his eyes firmly fixed on her half-naked body, she became painfully aware of how utterly on show she was.

He stood back, undoing the knot of his tie and unbuttoning his shirt slowly. Nicole's throat dried as his deliciously bronzed skin was revealed inch by inch, before he removed the shirt completely and dropped it to the floor.

'Do you want me to fold that up?' she asked coyly, unnerved by the crackling tension. 'We wouldn't want it to crease.'

'No jokes, Nicole,' he growled, grabbing her by the waist and holding her against him.

'I'm nervous,' she admitted, her voice barely a whisper.

'*Dio*, how can you not see how beautiful you are?'

'You're the only person to ever actually make me want to believe that.'

'That sounds like a challenge, *tesoro*.' His eyes gleamed.

CHAPTER SEVEN

SHE REACHED OUT, boldly running her hand across his bare chest, just as she had done that very first night in Paris a lifetime time ago. Only that time the room had been too dark for her to appreciate his perfection. Right now the faint glow of the candles bathed the room in just enough light.

Her sense of exposure intensified, but with his eyes locked on hers and the heat she saw there some of her self-consciousness melted away. He was just as turned on as she was— just as wild with anticipation as he seemed to drink in every inch of her body. She leaned her head back, closing her eyes as he ran his hands down her body. He cupped both her breasts, teasing her hardened nipples through the silk and lace of her delicate bridal corset.

The structured silk garment had originally

been designed for practicality, not seduction. But as Rigo turned her around and she caught a glimpse of herself in the mirror she began to understand the appeal of such feminine lingerie. She watched his eyes darken as he slowly pulled the laces loose. The fabric brushed against her already sensitive breasts as the whole thing loosened and came to rest around her hips.

Rigo moved against her, the heat of his erection pressing on her lower back as his tongue licked a path up from the sensitive spot between her neck and shoulder. Their eyes met in the mirror as his fingers explored her bare breasts, and Nicole couldn't resist moving herself back against the hardness of him.

Her hand seemed to reach down of its own accord to touch him through the fabric of his trousers. The pace of his breathing increased as she squeezed his length, then ran her fingernails down the hard ridge of his erection. The sound of his guttural moan filled her with pleasure, and her own heartbeat was now thumping powerfully in her chest.

Rigo suddenly grabbed her hand, pulling her with him across the room to the king-size four-poster bed. He sat on the coverlet and positioned her so that she stood facing him, trapped between his thighs. Her corset was dropped to the floor entirely, followed swiftly by her underwear.

Nicole instinctively moved to cover her abdomen, knowing that the faint marks from her pregnancy were now in full view for him to see.

Rigo moved Nicole's hands away, holding them by her sides as he looked his fill.

'Don't hide yourself from me.'

He leaned forward, taking one taut nipple in his mouth, his hands roaming on a path down her sides to cup her behind. And what a behind it was, he thought as he squeezed tight.

Nicole began to relax, her body leaning into him as he kissed a trail between her breasts. She was unsure of herself, of her appearance. Why, he had no idea. He couldn't make it any clearer how sexy he found her, how ridiculously turned on he was.

So he stopped talking, instead focusing on showing her with his tongue, running it down her abdomen. With the way his hands caressed the front of her thighs, spreading them apart so that he could stroke his knuckles along the soft dark hair between. He slipped one fingertip inside the crease to tease her with gentle touches before running a smooth rhythm up and down the crease of her lips.

Every one of her husky moans made it harder and harder not just to bury himself deep inside her and end the torture. He settled for moving a finger to her slick entrance, sliding it deep and setting a slow rhythm before adding a second. Nicole groaned deep in her throat, whispering something incoherent as he continued pleasuring her.

He bit hard on his lip, knowing he was the only man who had ever brought her this kind of pleasure. She was destroying his control with her unschooled responsiveness. There was no pretence in the way she dug her fingernails into his shoulders and let a harsh breath hiss out from between her teeth as her climax began to build.

He felt her muscles tighten and slowed his pace, wanting to draw out the torture a little longer. He had waited long enough to want to take his time. He wanted to tease her right to the brink, then feel her come apart on his tongue. Without hesitation he moved her back a pace and dropped to his knees in front of her. She didn't have a moment to protest before his tongue was sliding against her centre, stroking her in long, slow movements in time with his fingers.

Nicole grabbed a fistful of his hair as she moaned her release, each delicate spasm sending tremors against his tongue as he rode it out with her. He stood up, then laid her down on the bed, covering her body with his. She felt like hot silk… A man could drown in pleasure like this. It was like nothing he had ever felt and they had barely even got started.

She opened her legs for him, pressing herself against his erection without any of the nerves from earlier. A good orgasm apparently made his wife brave. He smiled to himself. He must make note of that for future reference.

He lowered his mouth to hers, kissing her hard and deep, knowing she could taste herself on his tongue. That fact only served to make him harder as he lay back on the bed beside her and grabbed her by the waist. He wanted her on top of him, so that he could watch her as he made them both come.

Nicole tensed, her hand on his chest as she half leaned over him. 'Rigo…' She bit her lip, her voice hesitant.

'Just trust me.' He pressed a kiss to her lips, holding her waist and guiding her on top of him so that her thighs cradled his hips completely. He held his breath as she slowly lowered herself to him, capturing his erection in a vice-like grip of molten heat.

Rigo head tilted his head back against the pillow, the sensation of delicious tightness almost more than he could bear. Nicole lifted her hips slightly, sending fresh waves of pleasure up his spine.

'*Yes*—just like that,' he urged, groaning as she repeated the motion and circled her hips in a slow, tortuous rhythm.

From this angle he had a full view of every tantalising curve of her body. The full high peaks of her breasts, the inward curves of her waist. She was like something that had walked straight out of his wildest fantasy. He took a moment to relish the fact that she was entirely his. The knowledge that he had been the only man to see her this way, to feel her as she lost control of herself…

He sucked in a breath as she leaned over him, giving him the perfect opportunity to claim her breasts once more. She was fast gaining pace, sliding against him in a steady rhythm as she braced her hands on the bedposts above them. Rigo thrust upwards in time with her, feeling his pleasure intensify. He had never felt an orgasm build this slowly, seeming to thrum up the tension in every nerve ending of his body.

He took one of her hands from the bedpost and guided it to her clitoris. 'Show me how you like it…'

Nicole's eyelids fluttered down as her fingertips drew a slow circle on her clitoris. Knowing he was watching her touch herself was both shocking and intensely sexy. She forced herself to open her eyes, to look down at him as she brought them both closer to their release. The pleasure was so intense she almost stopped, her breath coming hard and fast as she rode him.

Rigo seemed to sense her uncertainty.

'Harder,' he growled, sinking his fingertips into her hips.

He thrust upwards, filling her so completely that she cursed. His eyes widened, and his hands tightened on her hips as he repeated the motion, over and over. She could tell that he was close—just as she was. Her fingers worked faster. Her orgasm was building with such intensity it took her breath away. When she finally shattered into a million pieces Rigo wasn't far behind her. A few sharp thrusts were all it took for his muscles to tighten beneath her and spasms to ripple through his powerful body.

Nicole tried to move, not wanting to collapse on top of him, but Rigo kept his grip on her hips. He groaned low in his throat as he buried his mouth in the valley between her breasts and pulled her down to cover him. She relaxed her muscles, unable to hold herself up any longer, and gloried in the aftermath of their lovemaking.

'I have been thinking about doing that for weeks,' Rigo whispered in her ear. 'Watching you ride me while you touch yourself...'

Nicole shied away from his erotic words, her bravery fast waning.

He nipped the skin just below her ear, his voice a low rasp. 'You have no idea what it does to me to have you in control like that…' His words were slurred with tiredness as his body turned so that they lay on their sides, his arm around her waist, holding her close against his chest.

Nicole heard the moment his breathing slowed and sleep claimed him. She felt his heat surrounding her, protecting her, and as she looked down she caught the glint of his gold wedding band in the dim light. After all the pleasure she had just experienced she had almost forgotten that they were married. She was someone's wife now.

And this man—this utterly sinful, passionate man—was her husband. The concept of man and wife had never truly held any weight with her until today. But as she had stood in the church and made a vow to love and honour the man beside her she had been jarred by an errant thought.

She wasn't quite sure if she had been acting.

Rigo lay on his stomach, his face completely relaxed in sleep and mere inches from hers.

Nicole had no idea what time it was, but judging the brightness of the sun at the windows it was late morning. She turned on her side, taking in the sheer presence of him. A strange tingling sensation began in her stomach as she raked her gaze down over his muscular shoulders, over the smooth olive-toned skin that lay bare down to his hips before being covered by the soft white sheets.

If she moved her foot ever so slightly the sheet would slip down further, revealing just a little more… She bit her lip, smiling at her own wayward thoughts.

She tested her theory, shifting her foot and watching as the sheet slipped down an inch. One tanned, toned buttock was revealed and she felt her breath catch. Her eyes darted up to his face. Thankfully he was still sleeping. Her throat was painfully dry, her heartbeat quickening, but still she got braver. With one smooth flick she pulled her foot away completely. The sheet came away, too, bringing every hard, muscular plane into view.

His body shifted suddenly, and Nicole froze as his muscles flexed before his entire body turned so that he lay on his back. She looked up, and sure enough he was wide-awake, watching her with a mischievous glint in his eyes.

'Please, by all means carry on. Don't let me disturb you.'

Rigo's husky drawl made her cheeks warm as he reached out to stroke a hand lazily down her ribcage.

Of course, him being on his back now meant that an entirely different plane of muscles was on show. Nicole looked away, focusing instead on his face. His eyes were crinkled at the sides with the effort of holding in his amusement.

'I have absolutely no idea what the etiquette is for this situation.' She looked up at the ceiling, trying not to smile herself.

'This is new territory for me, too, Nicole.'

She looked back at him, one brow raised. 'Oh, come on—you've probably done the "morning after" routine so many times you've lost count.'

'None of those women were my wife.'

She was his wife.

Nicole's brain seemed to trip over the words uncomfortably. It all just seemed so surreal. Here she was, lying in bed with him after a night of the most intense lovemaking she had ever experienced. Granted, it had only been her second time, and with the same guy. But still…

She bit her lip. 'We should probably talk about how this affects…everything.'

'Is that what you want to do?' he asked.

He was looking at her with a gaze so heated it made her skin prickle. He rolled over, pushing her down to the bed and covering her body with his own. His skin was deliciously bed warm, and hard against her. She realised she had been waiting for him to do just this—that her body had been craving contact with his from the moment she'd opened her eyes.

'If you want to talk, by all means go ahead. But I can't promise I'm going to pay attention.'

His head bent down to trail kisses past her collarbone. Nicole felt the scorching heat of his tongue make a trail down the sensitive underside of her breast. He wasn't playing fair at all.

'I'm just not sure what we're doing, that's all…' she breathed, groaning as his tongue darted across her nipple in one harsh flick.

'Clearly I'm not doing it correctly.'

His gaze held hers captive as he took her whole nipple into his mouth, caressing it with his tongue and lips until she moaned low in her throat. He moved her legs apart, settling his body between her thighs. He fitted perfectly there, the dark hairs on his abdomen trailing down to where his erection pressed, hot and heavy. She looked up at him, finding his eyes trained on her.

'I want you, Nicole.' His voice was a husky whisper. 'God help me, but I want my wife in my bed. I can't think of anything but having you underneath me, crying out with pleasure.'

He moved a fraction of an inch. She sucked in a breath as the tip of him slid ever so slightly against her most sensitive spot. Her eyes drifted closed. The delicious pressure was taking over.

'Look at me,' he said, lowering his body weight onto his forearms so that his chest lay against hers. 'Tell me that you want this.'

It wasn't a demand, but also not quite a question. She urged her sex-hazed brain to respond, but couldn't find the words. Every inch of her skin was being burned up with his heat. Her legs rose to grip his hips, silently begging him to end the torture. He was still waiting, watching her intently.

'I want this,' she whispered, pulling his head down to close the final gap between them.

Her kiss was hungry and filled with the need that consumed her. He was just as out of control. She could feel it in the way his shoulders trembled under her touch. This felt different from last night somehow. Maybe it was the light of the day that made it more real.

She forced herself to open her eyes as he pulled away, grabbing a foil pack from the bedside cabinet and sheathing himself.

His eyes never left hers as he entered her. Her body stretched and moulded to him, heat filling her and travelling up in waves across her abdomen. The angle of his erection sliding against her seemed to increase the pleasure almost to breaking point. It was overwhelming and yet not enough, all at the same time. He lay flush against her, his mouth and tongue devouring hers as he moved his hips in a slow rhythm that was blissful torture.

Nicole felt the tension in her sex building, felt the pleasure radiating through her in long waves but not quite seeming to crest. She clutched a fistful of the hair at the nape of his neck, willing him to go harder, to end the torture. Rigo kept his pace, his face buried against her neck, whispering something she vaguely recognised as Italian.

When she finally reached the peak she fought the urge to sink her teeth into his shoulder as molten heat coursed through her body in magnificent waves. With one final thrust he sank himself deep inside her and groaned his own release.

Rigo smiled as Nicole released her death grip on the armrest as soon as the 'fasten seat belts' sign was switched off. The bright light in the cabin seemed to exaggerate her pallor as she leaned her head back and exhaled softly.

The child, on the other hand, had been asleep in her car seat since they'd arrived at the airport an hour before. Nicole had anxiously confided her worries over cabin pressure to the stewardess, but he could see now that her worry was only partly about Anna.

'You are a nervous flier?' He raised a brow, thanking the attendant as she laid down two glasses of sparkling water and an assortment of light snacks.

Nicole moved to fuss over the blankets that cocooned the child, checking the belt that held the seat in place. 'I'm not usually, but it's Anna's first time on a plane.'

'And she is looking a damned sight better than you do right now.' He smiled. 'Relax, it's a short flight to Siena, and I assure you my jet is well maintained and completely safe.'

'I know that.' She forced a wan smile, letting out one long breath. 'I'm fine—honestly. I'm looking forward to getting a break from the publicity. That's enough to get me through this flight.'

'We won't be disturbed at the estate—that much I can guarantee.'

He had made sure to organise security for their stay, knowing that there were no real boundaries for the paparazzi. He had also arranged for the nanny to fly over for a few days, to facilitate some alone time with his new wife. He realised he was looking forward to taking some time off from work, and the thought made him pause. He had woken this morning more relaxed and satisfied than he had been in a long time. And yet on their drive back to Paris he had found himself tenser than ever.

The wedding photos had been on the magazine's website, setting off a storm of publicity he knew would be the final step in undoing any damage to the Fournier deal. The original scandal had all but disappeared from the most prominent tabloids once the news of their engagement had filtered through.

He looked down at his sleeping daughter, now legally a Marchesi by name as well as blood. He should be relieved that things were going to plan. The new developments in his relationship with Nicole would only strengthen their partnership—or so he hoped. She didn't seem the type to believe in the fairy tale of marriage. She had said herself that love was just a romantic notion, hadn't she?

He sat forward. 'Nicole, I was thinking about—' He stopped, noticing the faint yellow tinge to her cheeks. 'Are you sure you're okay?' He leaned across the table between them, pressing his hand to her forehead. She was cold and clammy.

She pushed his hand away, shaking her head as she took another deep breath, this time groaning openly. Without another word she stood up and moved like lightning down the luxurious cabin, shutting the bathroom door behind her with a loud click.

Anna let out a small cry in her sleep. The commotion had been enough to disturb her. He silently willed the child not to stir, but of course her eyelids began to flutter before she opened her eyes wide and settled them straight on him.

He had chaired intense, high-risk meetings between multi-billion-euro corporations in the past. He had given keynote speeches in front of tens of thousands of people. But this... He winced as his daughter's face scrunched up and her eyes filled with tears. *This terrified him.* He stood as Anna began to sniff, the tears welling in her eyes as she looked up at him.

'I'm not your *mamma*—I know,' he said, feeling utterly ridiculous. She didn't understand a word he was saying.

The sniffs turned to sobs, and after a moment of indecision he hurriedly undid the seat belt and lifted the small bundle into his arms. She was light as a feather and fitted neatly against his chest. The cabin was cool, so he kept a blanket wrapped tightly around her. He was probably doing it all wrong, but at least she wasn't crying anymore. He smiled as he felt a tiny fist grab on to his shirtfront. Two perfectly round blue eyes took him in, unapologetically curious.

The bathroom door opened and Nicole emerged, looking slightly less pale. She stood frozen for a moment, watching him with a strange look on her face. As soon as the baby caught sight of her *mamma* she was wriggling and craning away from him. Nicole made quick work of taking her into her arms and holding her close.

'Sorry about that,' she said quietly. 'I suffer from travel sickness from time to time. The worrying probably didn't help.'

'It's fine. I seem to have avoided breaking her for the time being.'

Nicole smiled, hugging Anna close to her chest. 'She's quite sturdy now, really. She was actually five weeks premature—you should have seen her when she was born...'

Nicole's voice died away, her words hanging between them, heavy and uncomfortable. Then Anna laughed, reaching up to grab a handful of her mother's dark hair.

'I should probably go and freshen up,' Nicole continued awkwardly. 'I'll take her with me this time. You probably have work to do.'

Rigo nodded, glancing at from his emails onscreen as she gathered up a bag of toiletries and disappeared into the bedroom at the back of the plane. Something dark and uncomfortable began to uncoil in his chest.

She was beautiful, his daughter. How he hadn't seen the resemblance straight away he would never understand. But the mind played cruel tricks when it was angry, and he had most definitely been angry. He had missed so much already. He wondered if the little girl would somehow have already erected a great big wall between them. Or if she would remember his absence and think of him forever as somehow lacking as a father.

As Rigo stepped out onto the veranda of his Tuscan villa he was once again filled with a sense of bone-meltingly deep calm. He nursed a cup of freshly brewed espresso in his hands and sat down to watch as pink fingers of sunlight spread across the dawn sky above the vineyards. The villa sat on acre upon acre of sprawling lush green hills and farmland. He listened to the glorious absence of traffic noise, pedestrian voices and all the other sounds he associated with his life in Paris.

Nicole appeared beside him, dressed in only a light silk robe, her hair spread over her shoulders in a tumble of loose errant waves. He had made love to his wife once more in the night, after waking to feel her long limbs tangled with his own, and then again just before they had decided to get up early for breakfast.

'This view is breathtaking.' She sighed, leaning forward against the balustrade as she cradled her own steaming cup of coffee in her hands. 'If it were mine I would never leave.'

'Technically it *is* yours now.' He stirred his coffee thoughtfully. 'I bought this place to help drum up profit in the local area, with the vineyards and the stables, but I don't think I've set foot here more than twice in the past few years.'

'Don't you ever take time off?' she asked. 'Wait—I already know the answer to that question.'

'I live a very busy life, as you know. But I

have been ordered by my PR team to take this honeymoon so I plan to make the most of it.'

'You make it sound like such a chore.' Nicole's expression dropped a little, her eyes drifting away to gaze out at the sudden sparkling fountains of water that had begun to fly through the air as the sprinkler system began to drench the land.

'I'm sorry if my lack of enthusiasm offends you, but I'm simply not built to be idle. It makes me feel edgy.'

She looked up at him. 'That's possibly the first spontaneously personal thing you've ever said to me,' she said. 'I was beginning to wonder if you might be made of stone under all that muscle.'

'I think we both know that I don't run cold with you, *tesoro*.' He reached out to trap her in the circle of his arms, pulling her close.

Nicole laid her coffee down on the table beside them, placing her hands flat on his chest. 'We communicate well in bed—that much is true. But I'm talking about when we're not in bed, Rigo. It makes me uncomfortable to think that you know practically everything about me while I still know so very little about you.'

'What would you like to know?' he asked, leaning back against the balustrade.

'I don't know.' Nicole laughed. 'That's like asking me how many grapes grow in this vineyard.'

'About five and a half tons per acre, give or take.' He smirked at her answering glare. 'I'm joking—that's just a guess.'

'Isn't there a Rigo Marchesi that you have never shown to the world?'

His expression faltered for a moment, and the emotion in his eyes was so intense it made her breath catch. But just as quickly as it had appeared it was gone, making her wonder if she had simply imagined it.

'I have never lived under any pretence like you have, Nicole. The Marchesis don't have the luxury of keeping secrets,' he said nonchalantly, taking another sip of his coffee. 'If you want to know more about my secret wine collection, now, *that* is something I can do.' He smiled—a brilliant expression that transformed the previous shadows in his face.

Nicole looked at his smile and felt something bloom inside her. That small little seed of silly hope that she knew she was clutching tight to her chest. He was still holding back a lot of himself. But was she naive to hope that their attraction might bloom into something deeper if given the chance? They would be here together for the next couple of weeks, and she was determined to make the most of her chance to dig under the protective armour he seemed to wear.

After they'd washed and dressed they spent the day exploring the grounds of the estate, with Rigo seeming more at ease holding Anna as he pointed to all the different types of grapes that grew in the massive vineyard.

Nicole tried her best to step back and let him take the lead. She hadn't expected him to be so interested in his daughter. She didn't want to get her hopes up that he would be an involved father when she had already seen how much he worked. But as Rigo leaned down and dropped a kiss on Anna's cheek she felt another layer of the armour around her heart crack apart. Anna nestled her face into his shoulder and Rigo's brows rose in surprise.

'I think she's starting to like me.' He looked to where Nicole stood, watching them.

She tried to laugh, ignoring the way her

heart soared at the sight of him holding his tiny daughter. That pesky glimmer of hope bloomed once more in her chest, making her want things she couldn't have.

Rigo sorted in the sight of him holding his tiny daughter. That rare glimpse of love blossomed over him, it refreshed nothing in him that thought she couldn't have

CHAPTER EIGHT

RIGO MOVED AWAY from the doorway after watching Nicole lay their daughter down. She had fallen asleep in her arms. The little girl was exhausted after a morning of paddling in the pool followed by an afternoon visiting the stables. The past week, since they'd landed in Tuscany, had passed for him in a comfortable routine of long days exploring the surrounding towns followed by long, hot nights with his wife.

Nicole followed him out to the veranda, plugging the monitor in nearby as Rigo grabbed two glasses of wine.

'I don't think I will ever settle for another wine again after tasting this.' Nicole sighed deeply, leaning her head back as they sat down on one of the loungers, side by side.

'All the wine from this vineyard is exceptional. But this particular one is from their vintage collection—my personal favourite.'

'So are you going to explain your behaviour earlier?' Nicole smirked, a knowing smile playing on her lips.

'You mean when I saved Anna from having her fingers bitten off?' Rigo shook off the sheer anxiety he'd felt at having the small child in the stables, surrounded by his huge stallions.

'The horse was at least two feet away, Rigo. And I was holding her tightly.'

'She was getting too excited—flapping her tiny fingers in front of it. It was only a matter of time before something happened.'

'Oh, Mr Serious, you really do need to learn how to relax.' Nicole tutted. 'Anna was in no danger today. You seem to have bonded with her a little over the past week. Am I sensing some kind of overprotective-father syndrome?'

'It's hardly overprotective to want to make sure she doesn't get hurt, is it? I mean, maybe I was a little over-cautious. But what was I supposed to do? Just let her have her hand bitten off?'

Nicole burst out with low laughter, her

shoulders shaking from the force of it. 'Welcome to parenthood, darling.' She smiled at him. 'One long endless road of worry and self-doubt.'

Rigo paused, absorbing her words. Was that what had been wrong with him today? The tension in his body at having his tiny daughter so close to the animals had almost driven him insane. In the end he had just herded them all back to the house so they could swim in the pool while he caught up on some emails.

Nicole had been pushing and pushing for him to spend more time with Anna, and he knew he was being unreasonable by keeping himself at a distance. So all week long he had tried to be more interactive—swimming and talking and trying to form some sort of bond. But he was beginning to think that maybe he just wasn't built for fatherhood.

'Rigo, can I ask you something?' she asked, turning to him. 'It's just something that's been playing on my mind after meeting your family and seeing you here with Anna.'

He nodded and took a sip of wine, waiting for the question he had known she would ask eventually.

'Why did you decide not to have children at such a young age?' She frowned. 'You come from such a tightly knit family, it just doesn't make sense.'

'Nicole…' he began, not quite knowing what to say. He didn't want to talk about the past—that was for sure. But the look in her eyes told him that she was serious about this.

'I just want to understand the man I'm married to. Is that so terrible?'

'I had a vasectomy because I came to the decision that fatherhood was not for me. Is that so hard to believe?'

'And now…?'

He paused. And now he could feel himself caring more and more for his wife and daughter every day. He'd spent this whole week with Nicole and Anna, doing various activities around the countryside. And each night he had lost himself in his wife's passionate embrace, making love to her until they were both spent. He had never slept so well as he had since coming to his villa. The place rejuvenated him. That could be the only answer for his sudden heightened sense of well-being.

Nicole was looking at him expectantly. He

took another sip of wine, eyeing her over the rim of his glass. 'I don't quite know what you want me to say.'

'Do you still feel the same about fatherhood now that you have Anna?'

'I didn't really have a choice, to be fair,' he said quickly, and then saw the hurt in her face. 'I didn't mean it like that.'

'Never mind. I don't know why I even bothered asking.' She sat back, turning to look at the still bright evening sky.

'I told you—I don't like to live in the past.'

'There's a difference between living there and pretending it never happened.' She looked at him. 'The night of the rehearsal dinner you mentioned having a fiancée before me…'

'If you insist on knowing ancient history, far be it from me to deny you.'

He put his glass down, clearing his throat. He felt his thumb begin to tap nervously on the side of his chair, and stilled the movement before it became too pronounced.

'Her name was Lydia. We met when I was in my final year of college in the States. She was a year older than me…worked in a coffee shop on campus. I met her at a bar one

Friday night and before I knew it we were living together.'

'That fast?' Nicole asked.

'Too fast. But I couldn't have known that at the time. I was too madly in love to see the warning signs all around me.' He stood up, walking over to perch against the balustrade of the terrace. 'We were barely together six months before she told me she was pregnant.'

Rigo took in a deep breath, hating the effect this was having on him. He hated thinking of that time in his life. When he had been so utterly young and naive.

'I was a romantic fool. I proposed instantly and flew us both here to meet my family. I didn't tell them about the baby, of course. That was to be our secret until after the wedding.'

He laughed—a cruel sound, deep in his chest.

'She had me wrapped around her finger. If my mother hadn't taken an instant dislike to her, who knows what way things might have gone? My mother arranged for some security checks—just a precaution before the wedding. I remained here while Lydia flew back to the States to continue the wedding plans. With my credit card, of course.'

Nicole looked up at him, her face tight with tension as he continued.

'I remember I was sitting outside the chapel after booking our wedding date when she called me, crying. She had lost the baby.' He shook his head. 'I sat on the steps of that church and I cried with her, utterly heartbroken for the life we had lost. I got on the next available flight and rushed to her side. I cared for her, comforted her. I told her we would try again—that I would give her as many babies as she wanted.'

He sighed.

'My mother arrived at my apartment unexpectedly a few weeks later. Lydia was at a spa. I'll never forget the look on her face as she told me about the security checks she'd had performed. I was furious. I almost ordered her out. But then she showed me a copy of a medical document from one month before. It had Lydia's name on it. And there was a picture of her from security footage. In an abortion clinic.'

Nicole clapped her hand over her mouth in horror. 'Rigo...'

'I confronted her the moment she got home. Naturally she denied everything until I showed her the proof.' He shook his head. 'She told me she was scared of having the baby, that she was worried it would make me love her less. But by that point my mother had already shown me the massive bills she had run up on my accounts and I had lost the lovesick blinkers that had blinded me to who she truly was.'

Nicole sat silently, processing the revelation that Rigo had once been in love. He had said that he didn't believe in love and romance, but clearly at that stage in his life he had. And this woman had stomped all over that.

He continued unprompted, his face a tight mask of hurt. 'When I was having her things removed from my apartment I found a safety pin at the bottom of the same drawer I used for my condoms. She had often urged me not to use protection, claiming she was on the pill. But I was rigorously safe, even then.'

'She got pregnant on purpose?' Nicole breathed.

'She admitted it all eventually—once she realised it was over. It was hard, seeing the pretence fall away and finding that she wasn't the person she'd said she was. She had lied about almost everything in order to take me in.'

'So you chose to get a vasectomy because of what happened?' Nicole asked, still struggling to get her head around it all.

'I got over the break-up soon enough—the anger helped. I graduated and moved back to Italy to start working for my father. I was so lost I just wanted to run wild, to party and sleep around to blow off some steam. But every time I looked at a woman I wondered if she was just like Lydia.'

He raised his brows, sitting down beside her heavily.

'I couldn't sleep with anyone for more than a year. It tortured me. Then I heard my uncle having a conversation with my father about his mistresses and laughing about how they often tried to get pregnant, not knowing he'd had a vasectomy.'

'So you went and got one, too?' Nicole said quietly.

Rigo shook his head. 'It wasn't so simple as that. I truly agonised over it. When Lydia first told me she was pregnant I was terrified, but fear soon paved the way for excitement. I had always wanted to be just like my father, you see.'

'You still went through with it, though?'

'Yes. I decided that I would never risk giving myself like that ever again anyway, so children wouldn't be a possibility. I had the procedure, and only had attachments with women I knew were career driven and independent. Nothing close to a gold-digger.'

'Until you met me.' Nicole looked up at him, feeling the emotion of his revelation sitting heavy on her chest. 'It's very clear to me now why you reacted to me the way you did that morning. I reminded you of her, didn't I?' Nicole said sadly.

'I was unnerved by my oversight, yes. But I know different now. I know the truth about your past.'

'And yet still you're determined never to let anyone in ever again?'

'Nicole…I told you this to help you understand me…'

'And now I do. Very clearly.' She stood up, walking as far as the balustrade before turning to face him. 'What happened to you was painful and scarring. I can't imagine how difficult it must be to trust a woman again.' She shook her head. 'But here we are, married a little over a week now, and I'm only just finding this out.'

'I should have told you before. But we had agreed to keep our distance, I didn't think you needed to know.'

'I thought that you were distant with me because of *our* past. That you were still learning to trust me. I've been hoping that maybe with time… That some day we could have more.'

'I do trust you, Nicole.' He stood up, taking her hands.

She shook him off, turning away. 'You trust me not to steal your money, perhaps. But you'll never trust me with your heart, will you?' She turned back, seeing his face twist in confusion.

'My *heart*? What does that have to do with trusting one another?' He raised his voice.

'Everything!' she said, emotion pouring out of her with every word. 'How can you not tell that I'm head over heels in love with you?' She refused to let the tears fall from her eyes. 'I've been falling for you since the night I opened up and told you about my past.

I spoke the truth for the first time and you listened. You're the only person in this world who truly sees me for who I am. What we have together is real—can't you see that?'

'I know it's real. We have a great thing here, Nicole.'

'But you don't love me.' She let the words fall heavily between them. Creating a gap that she knew now would never be filled no matter how hard she tried.

Rigo ran a hand through his hair, his blue eyes darkening with frustration. 'It's not that I don't—it's that I can't. You're asking for something from me that doesn't exist.'

Nicole shook her head. 'Of course it exists. You're not a robot just because you've been burned badly. You're afraid to give yourself fully to anyone, and I understand that.'

'Nicole, let's just take a breather here...' He took a few steps away from her, his body tense and unyielding.

'This conversation was always going to happen,' she went on. 'And I'm glad it's happening now. I won't settle for half a relationship—not when I know now that I deserve more.'

'So I don't deserve you? Is that what this

is? You're trying to force me to say things when you don't even understand what you're asking of me.'

'You don't have to say anything. I won't push you, or walk away in a storm of tears.' She cleared her throat. 'I'm giving you the option to go back to our previous arrangement.'

'Nicole…'

'That is all I'm prepared to give, Rigo. If we continue down this road someone will end up getting hurt. And we both know that someone will be me.'

Rigo remained silent, watching her with the coldest look she had ever seen him give. It was as though she could almost literally see shutters coming down in his eyes. Blocking him away from her words.

'I will still be your wife. But in name only.' Her voice was stiff and scratchy with the effort of holding off the flood of emotion she knew was imminent.

'If that's what will make you happy, then by all means move your things into one of the guest bedrooms.' He sat down, pouring himself another glass of wine.

Nicole stood there for longer than she

should have, staring down at the man she loved, willing him to come to his senses.

As she walked back indoors and moved silently up the stairs she willed him to follow her. Just as she had willed him to follow her on that day she had told him she was pregnant a lifetime ago. But this feeling was so much worse. Before, she hadn't loved him. She hadn't even known what love was. Now she felt as though her heart was breaking with every step away from him, even though she knew it was for the best.

She couldn't give everything to him knowing that he would never feel the same. That he would always be holding back some part of himself from her.

By the time she stood in their bedroom, packing her things into her case before moving them to another room, the tears had begun flowing in earnest. She continued to pack, wiping each tear away, furiously trying to hold it together.

Then she heard a loud engine roar to life outside the window and she looked down to see Rigo's car speeding down the driveway, its headlights disappearing into the night.

She sat down on the bed and finally admitted to herself what she had refused to believe completely. There was no hope to hold on to anymore.

Loud, whimpering sobs racked her chest as she leaned forward, wrapping her arms around herself.

It was over.

Rigo stood in the makeshift office at the villa, waiting for the call to tell him that his jet was ready to go. He still had five days left of his honeymoon, but he couldn't stay here a moment longer. Not now that Nicole was refusing to speak to him.

Her anger he could take easily. But her silence was more than he could bear.

He should have known it would end this way. Things had been going far too well. At least before they had been able to be civil at times. Now here they were, married a mere week and absolutely miserable, just as she had predicted. Divorce wasn't only a possibility now. It was inevitable.

He thought of his parents' marriage: thirty-five years strong without a single separation. How on earth did they do it?

He hadn't been able to find her all morning, but it was likely she had been collected by his parents' chauffeur and had forgotten to tell him. She had been regularly going to his parents' estate so that they could spend time with Anna.

They had probably spent more time with his daughter than he had at this point. He didn't know why he couldn't just be natural, like his father. Not that it mattered now. Once Nicole had left him completely he would probably only get limited visitation anyway.

The thought of them living apart from him filled him with emptiness, but he knew it was for the best. He couldn't give Nicole what she wanted. He would never be able to.

Nicole was fast regretting her decision to take Anna for a picnic without the stroller. The little girl's weight in her arms was like lead after a mere ten minutes of carrying her up the hill outside the villa. But the oppressive atmosphere in the villa was more than she could take. Rigo would be leaving today, and she didn't want to be there when he did.

She'd done enough crying over the past twenty-four hours to last her a lifetime. And it was time she got used to living here alone now that she had chosen to stay.

She loved this place. The views and the smells. It was the perfect place to raise Anna. The people here were used to the Marchesis, and they didn't bother them. It would be a quiet life.

She stopped at the top of the hill, finding a nice leafy tree for them to seek shade under. It was still early morning but it was already a balmy twenty-five degrees. She set about propping Anna on a blanket and kicking off her shoes. She had brought some fruit and bread as a midmorning snack, and laughed as Anna grabbed a piece of melon from her hand and sucked on it greedily.

She would be all right here, she told herself as she munched on her own fruit. She had her daughter and her privacy and that was all that mattered right now.

Once they had finished eating it was nearing eleven, and much hotter. She stood up, stretching her leg muscles from being cramped underneath her for so long. She looked further ahead of her, to the hill that led to the church. For some reason she felt suddenly unnerved by the quiet that usually calmed her.

A man was standing there, beside a black car, his face partially obscured by a wide straw hat. He looked like a local, she thought, her mind working overtime to process her sudden feeling of unease.

Without warning the man pulled a dark bag out of the car, unclipped a large telescopic camera and began walking down the hill towards her.

Paparazzi. Nicole didn't waste a moment. Abandoning her picnic and the blanket, she covered Anna's face and walked as fast as she could manage in the opposite direction. She looked over her shoulder, and sure enough the man was pulling out the high-scope lens and breaking into a run. Her heart beat hard in her chest as she fought to hold Anna close, still shielding her face.

She broke into a run down the hill but, having abandoned her sandals with their picnic, found her bare feet soon ravaged by the rough terrain. Every step proved to be pure agony as she tried frantically to stay ahead of her pursuer.

Her steps faltered as she heard a scuffling behind her. Turning to check he wasn't gaining on her, she lost her footing and caught her heel on a sharp rock. Anna began to cry—a sharp, piercing sound that sent waves of pain straight to Nicole's heart. The man was gaining on them—fast.

He didn't care if her daughter was terrified, she thought angrily. All he wanted was a million-euro picture of her child. There was no way in hell he was getting it.

Hissing with the pain, she stood straight and forced herself to put pressure on her foot, feeling tears prick her eyes. They were almost at the gates, she told herself. They were almost safe. She shouted for the security guards who stood sentry there, her voice shaking with adrenaline. Anna was crying in earnest now, her little body shaking as she clung to her blouse.

Mercifully the men responded quickly, running out of their hut to meet her. But they were quickly overtaken by the appearance of her husband, his face a mask of pure rage.

CHAPTER NINE

RIGO'S FIST CONNECTED squarely with the photographer's fleshy jaw, sending him to the ground instantly, where he lay cowering. He grabbed the camera, hurtling it at the boundary wall of the estate with a satisfying smash.

'You're going to regret this, Marchesi.' The man spat blood onto the ground, groaning as he held his rapidly swelling jaw.

Rigo leaned down, grabbing him by the collar and watching him wince in preparation for another punch.

Nicole's hand on his arm was the only thing that stopped him from pummelling the man to within an inch of his life. The red rage lifted and the sound of his daughter's terrified cries was suddenly all he could hear.

His security guards stepped in, pulling the man to his feet and holding him in their grasp while one began contacting the local law enforcement.

Rigo reached out, taking Anna from Nicole's shaking arms. The little girl nestled into him, her cries still fearful but not as piercing now that he held her close. Holding Nicole by the arm, he guided her away from the ugly scene, back towards the villa as his heart hammered painfully in his chest.

Once inside, Rigo calmed Anna with quiet shushing until she was laughing once more. He set her down in her playpen and surrounded her with toys. He had to tend to Nicole's injured feet. The sight of her panic-stricken face flashed through his mind, making his fists clench. He blocked it out. Needing to do something practical to calm himself, and to stop himself from running out and physically attacking the rat once more, he grabbed a first-aid box from the kitchen, getting to work cleaning her raw wounds and bandaging the more open cuts.

Nicole hissed with pain. 'I lost my shoes when I ran from him.'

Rigo clenched his jaw. 'He's going to be taken care of—don't worry.'

'He's going to sue you for attacking him,'

Nicole whispered, looking past him to the windows.

'I'd like to see him try,' Rigo gritted, putting one last rub of salve on her skin before closing up the kit with a dull click.

He stood up, needing to move, needing to rid himself of the awful sensation of his control slipping further and further away. He had acted rashly in punching the bastard, but he would do it again—countless times.

'Rigo, this is bad.' She looked up at him. 'You have basically just started a war with the very people we've worked so hard to sway.'

'Would you have preferred that I let him walk away with pictures of our child?'

'No, of course not.' She winced as she put pressure on her foot. 'I'm just worried about how this will affect your deal…your company.'

Rigo's chest tightened. He hadn't been thinking about the company at all. If he was honest with himself he hadn't thought about it in days. He had acted on instinct, protecting what mattered most to him. For the first time in his life that hadn't been his own interests or the bottom line. When had Nicole and Anna become more important?

He stood up, pacing away from her to the window. In the distance he could see the repugnant photographer being bundled into a *polizia* car. Alberto stood at the gate, turning to look up at him with an expression he knew mirrored his own.

He had messed up—royally.

Nicole sat in the breakfast nook the next morning, watching as Rigo paced on the terrace and continued his phone call with the legal team. It unsettled her that she didn't know whether to reach out to her own husband or leave him be. Seeing him lose his temper so completely yesterday had been terrifying—like watching a stranger.

He returned inside, laying the phone down on the counter with a click and taking a long sip of his espresso.

'The photographer has started a lawsuit,' he said, clenching his fist tightly on the counter. 'He is claiming that because he was on a public road he should have had the freedom of the press. The media are pressing to have our injunction turned around.'

Nicole's hand froze, her croissant dropping back to her plate. 'He can't do that. He's just one man.'

'It's never "just one man" when it comes to the paparazzi and what they see as their God-given right to give the public what they want.'

Nicole felt suddenly cold, even though the morning sun shone in brightly through the windows. If their injunction was overturned it would mean that every detail about their relationship, their child, would be fair game.

'We will need to leave for Paris immediately,' he said, turning back to her, his hands thrust deep into his pockets.

'I am *not* going to Paris.' Nicole looked at him in amazement that he could even suggest such a thing.

'We need to tackle this, Nicole. If the Fournier deal falls through now thousands of jobs will be at stake. Not to mention the effect it will have on the Marchesi Group.'

'Your company is not my priority right now.' She bit her lip hard.

'Nicole, I need you by my side if we're to stand any chance of braving this,' he said earnestly. 'You're my wife.'

'Exactly. I'm your *wife*. So stop thinking

of me as a media device and consider my *feelings* for a change.' She stood up, ignoring the pain it brought. 'That man chased me down a hill to get pictures of my child, Rigo. Do you have any idea how terrifying it is to know that I still can't protect her?'

Rigo raised his voice. 'You agreed to this when you married me. You knew what a high-profile relationship involved.'

'I didn't agree to walking right into the heart of a fresh scandal. I can't go back to Paris. I can't put myself back out there for you. I'm sorry.' She shook her head, walking into the living room.

Rigo followed her, backing her up against the door. 'I did what I did to protect my family. I stood up for you. And now you are running away like a coward.'

'You know…that's exactly what my mother always said whenever *she* had done something that made my life more difficult,' she spat, and saw him react as though she'd slapped him.

Rigo frowned. 'That's unfair. You know that I care about you—and about Anna.' He stepped away from her, giving her some breathing room. 'I need you both with me in Paris, and that is final.'

'If you cared about us you wouldn't make us leave this estate ever again.'

'Nicole, listen to me. I will protect you both from the media.' He took her hands in his. 'I made that vow and I have already proved that I meant it. Let me protect you.'

Nicole shook her head sadly. 'You can't use me again and again to protect your company from scandal and still make out as though you're putting family first.'

He dropped her hands hastily, stepping away as though she'd burned him. 'So what? You're going to hole yourself up here and raise my daughter alone in this house like bloody Rapunzel? You think *that's* better than risking a photo of her being leaked?'

Nicole remained silent. Refusing to look at him.

He shook his head with finality. 'The only person being unreasonable here is you. I hope you're happy here in your own personal prison.'

He stormed out, leaving Nicole to stare at the door blankly.

Rigo remained completely silent in the conference room as all hell broke loose around him. The PR team had worked furiously for three days now to uphold the injunction, but with the story gaining steam on social media it had become akin to holding sand in their bare hands. The paparazzi were banding together, demanding blood, and the story was making waves across the globe.

Nobody cared that the man had ambushed his wife and child. He had been on public land and therefore within his rights. The fact that a billionaire had assaulted him and damaged the property of one of the 'little guys' was far more interesting than a case of child protection. The case would go to court, and the directors at Fournier had already called for an emergency meeting with the board.

They were going to jump ship, and there was nothing Rigo could do to stop his entire world from unravelling.

If only Nicole had trusted him enough— maybe together they could have swayed the public in their favour. But instead she had chosen to stay hidden away.

'Rigo, are you even listening to this?' The senior director of his legal department was looking at him expectantly, along with the rest of the room.

He sat up, suddenly very tired of the whole situation. All these people had been working tirelessly for him, likely neglecting their loved ones in the process, and all for what? These past five years had been devoted to growing his family company into the biggest fashion corporation in Europe. He had absorbed countless smaller companies, and with each one he had felt that same rush as when he'd first pursued Fournier. Now, with the deal set to crash and burn spectacularly, he felt nothing but emptiness.

The realisation than he no longer cared was so unsettling that he stood up and left the meeting without a single explanation, ignoring the shouts of concern as he shut the door behind him and ordered the car to take him home.

The drive through the busy streets of Paris passed in a blur. His mind was foggy and he felt subdued—likely to do with the fact that he hadn't slept or eaten properly in the days since he'd returned to Paris.

As the car pulled up to the kerb he noted the gangs of photographers still camped outside his apartment building. The abuse he had endured from their angry mouths for the past three days had opened his eyes to the kind of life Nicole must have lived. As Rigo Marchesi, golden boy CEO, he had never known anything but professionalism from the press. But now, branded a paparazzi attacker, he was subject to threats, taunts and worse from these men and women who hounded him day and night.

It was an eye-opening experience.

He entered his apartment, immediately noticing the vibrant blue fedora that lay on the kitchen counter. His father sat on the sofa, nursing a brandy, and looked up as Rigo walked into the living area.

'I came straight here as soon as I saw the news.' He stood up, pouring a second glass and handing it to his son with a half-smile.

'Aren't you meant to be in the rainforest somewhere right now?' Rigo raised a brow. 'Or did Uncle Mario send for you the minute he realised how badly I'd messed up?'

'Mario did call.' Amerigo nodded, looking down at his glass. 'But I'm here for my son— not for the CEO of the Marchesi Group.' He sat back, eyeing Rigo intently. 'Before this wedding, when was the last time you took a break, huh?' he rasped.

'I've got bigger things to worry about than that right now.'

'Another vital acquisition, I heard?' The older man shook his head. 'I admire everything that you have accomplished, Rigo. You have brought our family business to levels I never dreamed of achieving myself. But when is it going to be enough?'

Rigo looked at his father blankly. 'If everyone stopped after a certain level of success the world would grind to a halt. I believe in constant progress.'

'Progressing? Is that what you think you're doing? Because from here it just looks as if you're running on the spot.'

'Papà, I'm under a lot of pressure right now and I don't appreciate your taunts,' he gritted.

'You *need* to be taunted every now and then. You're so bloody stubborn—just like your mother...' he mused. 'Ever since that damn girl took you for a ride you've been like this. Running and running from the pain.'

'I have been getting on with my life. Why is that so hard to believe?'

'Because it's absolute crap.' His father sighed. 'And once you realise that maybe you will finally get over yourself and see that it is more important to leave this mess to fizzle out and go and enjoy the rest of your honeymoon. The company will survive the loss of Fournier.'

'It's not that simple.' He took a long swallow of the amber liquid and felt it scorch his throat. 'If I lose this deal the board will react. They have already expressed their anger.'

'Son, if I could impart to you one life lesson, it's this. Don't waste valuable time on what the board or anyone else thinks you should do. Live your life.'

His father's words echoed in his mind long after he had left him alone with his thoughts. He had told Nicole not to let the media dictate her life, but here he was, doing the very same thing. He had told her to trust him, that he would protect her from her fears. And yet the moment things got tough he had asked her to throw herself under a bus for his company.

He had treated her no better than her mother had for all those years and the realisation made him suddenly nauseous.

As the town car rolled slowly along the streets of Paris, Nicole wondered for the millionth time if she was doing the right thing.

Once she had heard that the court case was today she'd known she couldn't stay away any longer. She had to try to do something.

She stepped out of the car and looked up at the steps of the courthouse, seeing Rigo standing near the top, finishing up his statement to the press. He stood alone as the cameras turned away to move towards the prosecution group, who had just emerged from the building.

She felt her stomach tighten as Rigo turned and saw her. She suddenly felt a lot less brave. His face tightened with surprise and he powered down the steps towards her, his eyes darting towards the cameramen, who hadn't yet seen her.

'What the hell are you doing here?' he asked harshly. 'Get back into the car *now*— before they see you.'

'I'm here to give my statement,' Nicole said. 'I'm here to stand by your side.'

'It's all over.' Rigo exhaled harshly. 'I paid them off and the case has been thrown out. If you had told me you were going to come I would have told you to stay exactly where you were.'

'In my prison?' she asked quietly.

'I was angry at myself when I said those words.'

He took her hand, looking down at her with such fierce sincerity she thought her heart might break.

'No, you were right, Rigo. I can't live my life running away and hiding from these people or my voice will never be heard. I can't teach my daughter to be fearful.'

'When I said those words all I was thinking of was myself. I've been living under a microscope for days now and it's already driven me halfway to madness. But it was my actions that got us into this mess and I will face it alone.'

'I'm not just here for you, Rigo. I'm here for me, too. To prove to myself that I'm strong enough to protect my daughter.'

'You *are* strong enough, Nicole. You are the strongest woman I have ever known.'

A cameraman turned, catching sight of the candid discussion he was missing out on, and soon the whole press camp was descending upon them.

'Last chance,' Rigo warned, his fingers holding in a tight grip on her arm, as though he wanted to haul her away from the crowd.

She looked up at him, her eyes gravely serious. 'No more running.'

The crowd of cameras and microphones surrounded them with an excited hum.

One 'respectable' news journalist took an immediate jab. 'Nicole, what have you to say on the allegations that your marriage is a complete sham?'

Nicole took a deep breath, remembering the speech she had prepared and memorised on the plane journey. The words seemed to swim in her head, moving just out of her reach for a millisecond, before she squared her shoulders and grabbed them with both hands.

'Marriage is a deeply private affair for my husband and I,' she began, 'and just because we both may have previously courted the media it does not somehow make our private lives fair game.'

'What do you have to say about your husband's ferocious attack?'

'My husband acted instinctively, to protect my daughter and me from a stranger's harassment. I ask you this. In what world is it okay for a man to pursue a lone woman and an innocent child for the purpose of entertainment? Does his occupation give him the right to disregard the safety of those unable to protect themselves? Until my child is old enough to make the choice herself, I will be upholding her right to privacy.'

CHAPTER TEN

RIGO WAS IN awe of the strong, confident woman who stood poised on the steps of the courthouse. She held the media in the palm of her hand. Her words were unpractised, imperfect and deeply emotional, but they held all the more weight for it. What had begun as a press statement had somehow morphed into a public shaming of the paparazzi and their careless disregard for children.

He was seeing his wife transformed before his very eyes. Gone was the passive girl who had lived her life according to everyone else, and in her place was this fiery woman, poised and ready to wage war on those who dared to oppose her.

As she finished speaking a crowd of onlookers erupted into applause, and then the press began to ask more questions, one after another.

Rigo motioned to his guards to move forward as he carefully guided Nicole away.

'That was quite possibly the most terrifying, exhilarating thing I have ever done.' She smiled as they walked towards the street. 'I feel as if I could take on the world.' Her smile faded as he held open the door of his limousine. 'I'm not going with you, Rigo. I came straight from the airport,' she said quietly, gesturing to the town car parked just behind them. 'I'm flying back to Tuscany straight away.'

'We need to talk, Nicole. Please—just come back to the apartment with me.'

She shook her head. 'There's nothing else to say.'

'Nicole…'

Rigo fought past the strange tightness in his chest. He was trying to tell her how proud he was. How lucky he was to have her by his side. But the words wouldn't come, so instead he leaned forward and captured her lips with his. His hands tangled in her hair as he took his time, not caring about the people around them. He kissed her deeply, trying in vain to show her how much she meant to him.

When he ended the kiss she was breathless, and his chest was tighter than ever.

Nicole's eyes were guarded as she pulled away from him. 'Rigo…'

He held his breath as he watched her war with herself, but when she raised her eyes and he saw the solemn look in them, he knew the answer would be no even before she turned and walked away to her car.

As the pilot made his final checks Nicole took her seat and looked out the window with unseeing eyes. She should have just gone with him and drowned in his kisses. They would have gone back to the apartment under the pretence of talking and ended up falling straight into bed.

She bit her lip, swallowing past the lump in her throat that hadn't eased since she had walked away from him outside the courthouse.

She had told him that she loved him and he'd made it clear that he didn't feel the same. He cared about her. She knew he did. But she couldn't stay in a relationship in which she was the only one with both feet in the boat. Watching him walk away from her in Tuscany had broken her heart all over again, and she knew that she couldn't keep going round in circles when she was the only person who kept getting hurt.

There was a commotion at the door of the plane and suddenly the stairs were being lowered to the tarmac once more. Heavy footsteps banged hard on the steps and Rigo's hulking form appeared in the entryway.

'What are you doing here?' She unbuckled her seat belt and moved to her feet, facing him off in the bright cabin. The stewardess tactfully disappeared into the cockpit, giving them privacy.

Rigo stepped forward, his eyes dark with some unknown emotion. For the first time she noticed the dark circles under his eyes and the way his jaw was overgrown with dark stubble. Had he looked so tortured outside the courthouse?

'I shouldn't have kissed you like that.' His voice was deep with emotion as he fought to regain his breath.

Nicole crossed her arms. 'No, you shouldn't have.'

'I don't know what's wrong with me. It's

like I just keep saying or doing the wrong thing with you. Time after time.'

Nicole bit her lip, silently willing him to leave so that she wouldn't be tempted to forget why she'd left in the first place. 'There's no need to say anything. I told you to go and live your life separately.'

'That's the problem, Nicole.' He shook his head. 'I don't want to be anywhere else but right here with you.'

The air in the cabin seemed to thicken around them as his words echoed in her mind.

He continued, watching her intently. 'That day with the photographer, when I walked out and saw you terrified and bleeding, I swear to God something seemed to rise up and choke me from inside. I'm a grown man, and yet I was afraid of how utterly helpless that made me feel. You had already told me to either love you or leave, Nicole. But what I didn't realise is that I've been trying not to lose my mind over you from the moment I first saw you.'

'Rigo, I meant it when I said I wouldn't settle for half a relationship...' Nicole breathed, her mind swimming with the effect his intense gaze was having on her.

He closed the gap between them, taking her hands in his and making her look at him. 'I won't settle, either. I want it all, Nicole.'

This was an entirely different side to him than she had ever seen before. He was completely bared to her, saying things that she had only ever dreamed he might say. She didn't dare to speak, fearing she might break the spell.

'I was a complete fool to think that I had lost myself after my relationship with Lydia. The truth was I was shielding myself from ever being hurt like that again. Even from Anna.' He shook his head. 'I know I don't deserve it, after all I've done, but I couldn't let you get on this plane and fly away without taking a chance and risking rejection. I want to be your husband, Nicole, in every sense of the word. Let me love you like you deserve to be loved.'

'Are you telling me that you *love* me?' Nicole breathed, her heart soaring in earnest.

'*Tesoro*, I've been in love with you since the moment I slid that ring on your finger and made you my wife. I was just too much of a stubborn fool to realise it.'

Nicole felt her heart melt completely as she

looked into his deep blue eyes. She couldn't think of a single coherent thing to say. She settled instead for wrapping her arms around his neck and kissing him with all the passion she had to offer.

Rigo felt Nicole's lips touch his and his heart almost burst right then and there. He lifted her up from the ground, kissing her with all the love he possessed. She felt so good in his arms, so right. How had he ever thought he would be happier without this woman in his life?

The thought of how he had hurt her so many times made his gut clench. He broke the kiss and slid her down to the ground, smiling as she groaned in protest.

'Nicole, I understand if I have messed up too many times for you to trust me, but I want to make that right. If you give me the chance I promise I will never walk away from you again for as long as I breathe.' He laid his forehead on hers. 'I want to spend more time with my family and stop working myself into the ground.'

'You would do that for us?'

'For all three of us,' he said earnestly. 'I

never want to be away from my family for longer than I need to be.'

'Not even if I leave my underwear strewn all over the bedroom floor?' She raised a teasing brow.

'Especially then.' He smiled. 'I love you, Nicole. So much.'

'I don't think I'll ever get sick of hearing you say those words.' She draped her arms around his neck, nestling her face into his collar.

'I'M FINDING IT hard to adjust to the sight of my husband driving his own car.' Nicole smiled, resting on her hand on Rigo's forearm as he guided the SUV around another tight bend in the narrow French country road.

'I'm probably taking the concept of Sunday driving a bit too literally.' Rigo gestured to the leisurely speed on the digital panel. 'I chose luxury over speed, seeing as the Ferrari wasn't an option.'

He looked briefly over his shoulder and smiled.

Nicole followed his gaze to where Anna slept peacefully in her car seat. How had an entire year passed since she had first laid eyes on her baby girl? When she thought back to that day in the hospital, holding her daughter's tiny hand and wondering if Rigo had any idea he had just become a father...

Never in her wildest dreams would she have expected to be sitting next to him on their daughter's first birthday, married and planning a long, happy life together.

The object of her thoughts laid his hand on her thigh, jolting her from her smiling reverie.

'Do you recognise the road yet?' He raised a brow, a devilish smile on his lips.

Nicole shook her head and peered out at the rolling French countryside, trying in vain to spot anything familiar. They had headed away from Paris on one of the many motorways that wove in networks across the country. Her attention had been monopolised by Anna for the first half of the journey, so she had no idea where they were.

Rigo gestured to the road ahead of them, where a sign was appearing on the horizon. Nicole squinted, trying to make out the small black lettering. Suddenly her breath caught. Her eyes darted to her husband's face before flying back to the road as a tiny town came into view.

'You've brought me to L'Annique?' she whispered. 'Oh, Rigo...'

'I thought it would be a nice tradition to spend Anna's birthday here every year.'

Nicole fought against the wave of emotion rising in her chest as they passed the small church on top of the hill and looked down on the place that had been her first slice of normality. La Petite was the farmhouse where she had started to become her true self—where she had let go of the pretences of her old life and embarked upon a new adventure.

'You are a true romantic, Rigo Marchesi, do you know that?' She smiled, grabbing his hand and putting it to her face, feeling an overwhelming love for the powerful man by her side. 'We could have lunch in Madame Laurent's café. It's nothing special, but I used to eat there regularly.'

'Actually, I had something else in mind.'

He guided the car around a corner and began driving up a familiar road. The last time Nicole had seen this laneway it had been filled with paparazzi, but today it was blissfully clear and lined with beautiful summer wildflowers. The gate to her rented house came into view, along with the familiar blue-grey roof of the farmhouse that had been her home.

She fought the urge to jump with excitement when Rigo drove into the courtyard and brought the car to a stop. They stepped out into the glorious sunshine, and the familiar smell of cut grass and bluebells washed over her. This place was like a balm to her soul, reminding her of that first choice she had made on the path to becoming the woman she was today.

She walked over to the small fountain on the lawn and ran her fingers across the ageing stone. 'I'm not sure the owner would like us trespassing, but I'm glad you brought me here. Thank you, *amore*,' she whispered, walking back to lay a single kiss on his lips.

'Oh, I'm sure the owner won't mind,' Rigo said, turning to peer through the window of the car. 'She seems to be sleeping at the moment, but you can ask her once she wakes.'

It took a moment for his words to sink in to her love-clouded brain. Then Nicole looked up at him in disbelief. 'The owner is Anna? Wait…you *bought* the farmhouse?'

Rigo nodded once, gesturing to the grand old building. 'It's kind of her birthday present.' He smiled. 'I thought it could be our weekend getaway. Somewhere we can just be together. No housekeepers or chauffeurs. It's probably a little too extravagant for a first birthday, but...'

'It's perfect.' Nicole shook her head, feeling happy tears threaten behind her eyelids. Swallowing hard, she wrapped her arms around his neck. His eyes were so mesmerisingly blue in the sunshine that she almost forgot what she wanted to say.

He took her silence as a chance to continue. 'I remembered how fondly you spoke of this place and all the memories you'd made here together.' His voice trailed off, a strange look entering his eyes. 'I wanted to give that back to you—even if it reminds me of the time you both spent together without me. A time that I'm not proud of.'

'Rigo, you were always a part of this place.' Nicole sighed, stepping back and looking up at the picturesque whitewashed facade of her old home. 'A day never passed here when I didn't think of you, or talk to Anna about her *papà*. I had always planned to tell her about you some day.'

Rigo took a step towards her, taking her face in his hands. 'I hate to think of you here alone. Cursing me for being such a stubborn fool.'

Nicole looked up into the troubled eyes of the man she loved with all her heart. She knew he still struggled with missing the first months of his daughter's life.

'Rigo, our past is only there to pave the way for our future. Look at what we have now—look at the family we have built together. I for one wouldn't change a single thing.'

Rigo felt her words soothe the tightness in his chest. The look of pure love on her face made him hold her even tighter as he kissed her. It was one of maybe a thousand kisses they had shared since becoming husband and wife, and yet it was different. With this kiss the last piece of their past seemed to melt away, leaving in its wake only this one glorious moment. She was his and she always had been, from the moment he had taken her hand on that ballroom floor.

Rigo ended the kiss, looking back towards the open car door as a familiar gurgle could be heard breaking the calm. With a few strides he bent to scoop his daughter from her seat and deftly placed a small sun hat on her tiny head. Anna smiled up at him, her cheeks rosy from slumber. He had never expected for this to feel so right—holding his child in his arms and wanting to spend every moment of every day with her. But once he had given in to the overwhelming love his natural paternal instincts had soon followed.

'Happy birthday, *piccolina*.'

He dropped a kiss on Anna's cheek, wrapping his other arm around his wife. All that time he had spent trying to conquer the world from the boardroom meant nothing compared to holding his whole world in his arms at that moment.

'*Cent'anni,*' he whispered to them both. 'To a hundred years.'

* * * * *

Also available in the
SECRET HEIRS OF BILLIONAIRES
series

UNWRAPPING THE CASTELLI SECRET
by Caitlin Crews

BRUNETTI'S SECRET SON
by Maya Blake

LARGER-PRINT BOOKS!

GET 2 FREE LARGER-PRINT NOVELS PLUS
2 FREE GIFTS!

✦ HARLEQUIN®

Romance

From the Heart, For the Heart

YES! Please send me 2 FREE LARGER-PRINT Harlequin® Romance novels and my 2 FREE gifts (gifts are worth about $10). After receiving them, if I don't wish to receive any more books, I can return the shipping statement marked "cancel." If I don't cancel, I will receive 4 brand-new novels every month and be billed just $5.09 per book in the U.S. or $5.49 per book in Canada. That's a savings of at least 15% off the cover price! It's quite a bargain! Shipping and handling is just 50¢ per book in the U.S. and 75¢ per book in Canada.* I understand that accepting the 2 free books and gifts places me under no obligation to buy anything. I can always return a shipment and cancel at any time. Even if I never buy another book, the two free books and gifts are mine to keep forever.

119/319 HDN GHWC

Name	(PLEASE PRINT)	
Address		Apt. #
City	State/Prov.	Zip/Postal Code

Signature (if under 18, a parent or guardian must sign)

Mail to the **Reader Service:**
IN U.S.A.: P.O. Box 1867, Buffalo, NY 14240-1867
IN CANADA: P.O. Box 609, Fort Erie, Ontario L2A 5X3
Want to try two free books from another line?
Call 1-800-873-8635 or visit www.ReaderService.com.

* Terms and prices subject to change without notice. Prices do not include applicable taxes. Sales tax applicable in N.Y. Canadian residents will be charged applicable taxes. Offer not valid in Quebec. This offer is limited to one order per household. Not valid for current subscribers to Harlequin Romance Larger-Print books. All orders subject to credit approval. Credit or debit balances in a customer's account(s) may be offset by any other outstanding balance owed by or to the customer. Please allow 4 to 6 weeks for delivery. Offer available while quantities last.

Your Privacy—The Reader Service is committed to protecting your privacy. Our Privacy Policy is available online at www.ReaderService.com or upon request from the Reader Service.

We make a portion of our mailing list available to reputable third parties that offer products we believe may interest you. If you prefer that we not exchange your name with third parties, or if you wish to clarify or modify your communication preferences, please visit us at www.ReaderService.com/consumerchoice or write to us at Reader Service Preference Service, P.O. Box 9062, Buffalo, NY 14240-9062. Include your complete name and address.

HRLP15

LARGER-PRINT BOOKS!
GET 2 FREE LARGER-PRINT NOVELS PLUS
2 FREE GIFTS!

HARLEQUIN

super romance

More Story...More Romance

YES! Please send me 2 FREE LARGER-PRINT Harlequin® Superromance® novels and my 2 FREE gifts (gifts are worth about $10). After receiving them, if I don't wish to receive any more books, I can return the shipping statement marked "cancel." If I don't cancel, I will receive 4 brand-new novels every month and be billed just $5.94 per book in the U.S. or $6.24 per book in Canada. That's a savings of at least 12% off the cover price! It's quite a bargain! Shipping and handling is just 50¢ per book in the U.S. and 75¢ per book in Canada.* I understand that accepting the 2 free books and gifts places me under no obligation to buy anything. I can always return a shipment and cancel at any time. Even if I never buy another book, the two free books and gifts are mine to keep forever.

132/332 HDN GHVC

Name	(PLEASE PRINT)	
Address		Apt. #
City	State/Prov.	Zip/Postal Code

Signature (if under 18, a parent or guardian must sign)

Mail to the **Reader Service:**
IN U.S.A.: P.O. Box 1867, Buffalo, NY 14240-1867
IN CANADA: P.O. Box 609, Fort Erie, Ontario L2A 5X3

Want to try two free books from another line?
Call 1-800-873-8635 today or visit www.ReaderService.com.

* Terms and prices subject to change without notice. Prices do not include applicable taxes. Sales tax applicable in N.Y. Canadian residents will be charged applicable taxes. Offer not valid in Quebec. This offer is limited to one order per household. Not valid for current subscribers to Harlequin Superromance Larger-Print books. All orders subject to credit approval. Credit or debit balances in a customer's account(s) may be offset by any other outstanding balance owed by or to the customer. Please allow 4 to 6 weeks for delivery. Offer available while quantities last.

Your Privacy—The Reader Service is committed to protecting your privacy. Our Privacy Policy is available online at www.ReaderService.com or upon request from the Reader Service.

We make a portion of our mailing list available to reputable third parties that offer products we believe may interest you. If you prefer that we not exchange your name with third parties, or if you wish to clarify or modify your communication preferences, please visit us at www.ReaderService.com/consumerschoice or write to us at Reader Service Preference Service, P.O. Box 9062, Buffalo, NY 14240-9062. Include your complete name and address.

HSRLP15

CINELLI Amanda (ROMANCE)
Cinelli, Amanda.
The secret to marrying
Marchesi